I, Sarah Steinway

I, Sarah Steinway

—MARY E. CARTER—
A Novel

TOVAH
MIRIAM

Mary E. Carter
ISBN 978-0692985243
First Printing

TOVAH
MIRIAM

www.Tovah-Miriam.com • www.Mary-Carter.com

Other books by Mary E. Carter:

A Non-Swimmer Considers Her Mikvah
2016 WINNER New Mexico-Arizona Book Awards

A Death Delayed – Agent Orange: Hidden Killer in Vietnam, 2017

Electronic Highway Robbery, 1996

For Gary
And for my first teachers,
The Rabbis

All things pray...
pour forth their souls;
the heavens pray, the earth prays...
the flashes of the human mind
and the storms of the human heart...
are all prayers;
The wordless outpouring of boundless longing...

T'Filah Siddur Shabbat
Reform

-I-

In a place where there
are no human beings,
try to be one.

Pirke Avot 2:5

YOU WOULD NOT CREDIT IT AS SWIMMING. Flailing, more like. Too much thrashing of arms. Too much foamy kicking. She — I could see it was a female with my binoculars — she clutched a jagged shard of glass that jerked and flashed with her struggle. She sank several times and I could not help thinking 'good.' But then she would breech, up and out, her whole torso above the surface of the water. Gasping and spitting and heaving for air, she would plunge forward again, inching along toward my tree-house.

At one point, she rolled onto her back, floating, to rest I suppose. Panting and arching her chest a bit, she thrust the jagged glass between her teeth. It knifed into the corners of her mouth and sliced her cheeks. Blood flowed, a red grin, down into her ear canals.

The third planet from the sun rolled, dependable, through

space, welcoming another bright sunshiny morning. So lovely. Lovely little morning.

It was not like in the movies. I assure you.

This girl — really, she was just a girl, I could see that now — was swimming, struggling in the rising waters and she was energized. By what? Hunger? Anger? Insanity? Fear?

At last she dragged herself up my stairs, lurching toward my treehouse deck. She was bleeding, staggering, and armed with her shard of broken windowpane. Whipping it in front of her body, back and forth, slashing the air between us, this way and that way, ranting and grunting, she lunged closer to me with each thrust of her shaking arm. I understood that, intentionally or by accident, she would kill me or, at the very least, slice me with her weapon.

There had been a lot of killing in our world back before The Emperor Tides. When it came to murder, I would have thought that I had been well prepared to be quite indifferent to the act. Killing and murder were rampant in the last throes of our civilization, so-called. The surprise was this: when I was confronted with a dangerous, irrational, starving, crazy human being who was intent on killing me or, at least, on doing damage, I swung into action like a professional soldier. With all the skills that Jerry Sterns had taught me, acting on some level of instinct to live, I moved to stop this girl-swimmer.

Idiotically, I had not kept my pump action shotgun loaded. I edged across the floor, got within grabbing distance of it, lifted it to my cheek and racked the pump. It cracked. Loud.

And then she was gone.

Shaking violently, I vomited. I wept, jagged gasps, drooling long strands of my stomach contents onto my shirt. Still holding the shotgun, I had vomited on it too.

"You have your whole life ahead of you, Sarah."

No.

I do not have my life 'whole' ahead of me anymore, Danny.

Don't ask me about all this. Stop wondering.

Some nights it is all I can do to not think about murder and my stomach regurgitates my meager meal of fish and tea. With Jerry Sterns I had prepared myself to kill and, therefore, it was premeditated murder. Now, in addition to being a lone survivor, I was also beyond repair.

The person who I had believed myself to be — a person who was charming and thoughtful and discursive and sometimes even mordantly humorous — that old self was slashed to pieces as surely as I would have been if I had not murdered that first intruder, that girl. I realized on the morning of the girl-swimmer, that I could, from that day forward, shoot to kill. Or, rather, that I would shoot to live.

Long ago, in San Francisco, I had been happy and I had talked of love as if it mattered and talked of death as if it did not. Clasping Irish Coffee, I had been confident and arrogant and beautiful and stupid and twenty-one years old. Old enough to drink alcohol in public. But not old enough for much else.

Me, now.

My name is Sarah Steinway. As in piano. Seventy-five years of age I am, give or take. Lately I am called rabbi. When called. Which is not that often to tell the truth. But when, or if, I am called, it's a rabbi they will need. Let me be clear. I never did get the calling to be an actual rabbi; me, secular and all. Is that clear? I am NOT a rabbi. I don't even own a kippah. But circumstances have lately become so dire, so catastrophic, that even the word 'catastrophe' sits pale upon the page.

Why me, God?

When called, I am needed to recite the Kaddish. And to perform my rabbinic obligations, I wear a cowboy hat. Girl. A cowgirl hat. And me not even a cowboy. Girl. So, being neither rabbi nor cowgirl, I am neither fish nor fowl as we used to say. Although these days there are plenty of fish. More about this later.

How I got my cowgirl hat is that I dipped my bare hands into the racing flood waters and snagged it. I pulled it straight off the head of one of the nearby blobs of floating garbage. By this I mean: I stole my hat off one of the human, dead beings who floated past my treehouse after the big flood. The dead are merely detritus out here nowadays. And I could see that hat was nearly new. A Stetson. Such a waste it would have been, end of the world and all. I'm thrifty like that.

So, me being a rabbi, it was out of necessity, I tell you, and certainly way out of my control. Although, it turns out to be a happy coincidence that I did possess a hat. A Stetson, can you believe it? But most important to remember: I never volunteered. Is that clear?

Am I repeating myself?

How me being made a rabbi was that I was persuaded by a couple of genuine rabbis who came my way. Later for that story. Those traveling rabbis plied me with their special brand of rabbinic and Talmudic and learned conviction and all that. On the one hand, this. On the other hand, that. Their logic met my resistance. And so, I came round. Alright, already! So make me a rabbi!

Ah, yes.

Anyways.

My story is this: I live in a treehouse after a monumental flood. I have my books and some crazy gear given to me by some crazy survivalist — beautiful guy. I have a gun. Weapon. I know. I know. Never call it a 'gun.' My treehouse is built in the top branches of a California Live Oak. Firmly rooted, my tree overlooks what used to be the San Pablo Bay seasonal wetlands. That's at the top end of the San Francisco Bay. That beautiful legendary Bay and its attendant river wetlands are, sadly, no more.

I have lived up here — survived, I should say — several seasons now.

Why me, God?

You might recall that Robinson Crusoe lived on his island for more than twenty-three years. These things are possible. Like Robby, I eat, I work, I write. And on and on I go. Regular survivor I am. Me. Sarah Steinway.

I feed mostly on Slow Fish. These fish are some dynasty of finned creatures, created, dare I say, by evolution and hard luck. They are new since the flood and very handy for the stray survivor.

Anyways.

Slow fish: I named them that. Me. Just like Adam naming all the creatures on the land and in the deep. Slow Fish. I base this name on the fact that they are slow, very slow, and stupid, very. So all I have to do is scoop them up in my bucket when the tides are low. They die obediently and they are almost like anchovies. I eat them, bones and all and, since I am still here, a dubious distinction at this point, they must be nourishing. Yes? And here's a thought: they're kosher. I'm kosher! That's rich!

Anyways, now you know who I am. I better get on with my story. Everybody not dead yet most certainly will be, and soon. Me included.

One more thing — and I may be jumping ahead — but you'll thank me. I have an old typewriter up here. Gift of a friend. More on him later.

Here's the thing: I'm using my typewriter to tell you all about my life up here in my treehouse and you need to cut me some slack. I am not a writer. Not any more than I am a rabbi.

So here's the deal; you, whoever you are, need to know this about my typing, or, about my writing. Look. What I am writing about here, on my typewriter, is my life alone in my treehouse. I'm doing the best I can.

First off: when and if I talk to 'you', well it's just a habit, a way of speaking. You know?

And, as for when something happens to me, now or in the past, I just plunge ahead and keep typing. You need to just grab ahold and spin along with me.

Thus, you, the alert and well-read reader, might note that, sometimes, I slide between 'now' and 'then.' Between present events and past events. And, as if that weren't confusing enough, I talk like a past event is happening right now, before your very eyes.

You are discerning to notice this tendency. Kudos to you dear reader.

It's a slippery slope.

Work with me.

It's just that sometimes my mind veers off awkwardly from the literary style of the omniscient third person to, what I prefer to call, the first-person-furious.

"It was the best of times. It was the worst of times."

Is that the voice of God, whoever He, She, or It may be? Well, that's debatable. But it has become, I am told, the voice of literature.

Except that, this typing, which records my writing, is not literature.

Sometimes it goes like this: I am so immersed in reliving or referring to a past event in my life that I start talking, or typing, as if it were happening 'right now.'

Now it's happening! Right now! Help!

And suddenly, for example, you hear me shout to Daniel:

"No Danny, I do not have my life, whole, in front of me."

This is first-person-furious.

Then I shift back to third person, voice-of-God-kind-of-thing, or whatever it's called, and it just sounds right to my ears. I'm probably wrong.

And as for commas and semicolons and other bothersome nits, well dear reader, just pick them! I am doing the best I can.

So shoot me.

Anyways.

Here's what I recommend: you editors out there, just take it easy. Me, up here in my treehouse, surrounded by water, alone, I lose track, or don't care, about form and just shift, willy-nilly, between third person, voice-of-God sort of talk, and crazy-woman-yelling sort of talk.

So, sit back. Relax. Forget about Strunk. Take it easy all you sticklers for Chicago. Please let me, for God sakes, please, just let me speak for myself in whatever voice I'm inclined to use on any specific day of typing.

-II-

Sages, watch your words

lest you be punished

by exile to

a place of bad water.

Pirke Avot 1:11

THERE IS NO INFRASTRUCTURE NOW. No nothing out here now. No news. No Internet. No neighbors. No gossip. No lashon-hara — look it up. No sewers. No tap water. No cars, planes, skateboards. No concrete. Not now. Just water, deep and black. So how, I ask you, how can I tell you how these floods came to be? Or why? Or any of it? When these floods began, we had so little news to go on. And we were told it was all just 'fake news' anyhow. Even as the waters gurgled up higher and higher around our ankles, then up to our knees, all we got back then was home-tweet-homilies:

"It's all just stupid leaks! I'm surrounded by leakers! Bad!"

Feh!

You, who cannot go a single day without your computer, poking into news feeds, ten, twenty times a day, poor compulsive lab rat. Checking your email, rat at your lever, thirty times a day and not a crumb. Poor rat. Now: there is no nothing. And without my own support system of wires and digital miraculous devices, I can't tell you one thing that would be true and correct, about how The Emperor Tides began.

I can, however, brag that I have survived. Up here in my treehouse.

You either want to hear my story or throw these pages onto your bonfire; they'll keep you warm for an hour or so.

But stop. Stop I urge you. Stop wondering how this flood happened.

Sheesh.

Away! Go!

Just go away!

One thing for certain: I don't deserve credit for the 'good fortune' of my being still alive. Maybe it's just good stout DNA.

Stout DNA!

As if anybody around here envies good stout DNA these days. Nobody, if there is anybody, envies strong DNA at this point in The Emperor Floods. Or Tides. Or whatever you call them.

Oh well. Carry on. Just carry on. Time to gather another bucket of Slow Fish to keep starvation at bay.

At Bay! Ha! You love it? Puns lasting longer than plastic.

I stand out here on the deck of my treehouse. Facing east at break of day, I watch. Here are my conclusions:

Doesn't matter if you pray or don't pray. I've seen the pray-ers die and the non-pray-ers live. I have seen the believers die and the believers live. Then again, some pray-ers do live. Some non-pray-ers do die. Mox nix. Six to one, half a dozen, well, you know. Call out loud to God and you: A) Die. B) Live. Ignore God and you: A) Live. B) Die.

It's a wash. If you don't mind another pun on this damnable flood.

For me the floods started at Costco where the daily rising and ebbing of the tides made parking a problem. It slowly sunk in to my brain that, gee, maybe this was going to be bad someday.

In the early days, tides flowed inland, twice a day, two feet high along the San Francisco Embarcadero, a couple of feet in Larkspur, a few inches in Berkeley, two feet in San Rafael. You could still get to work, do your banking, have your sack lunch on the Justin Herman Plaza. Build a treehouse. It was all doable. Just.

The deep water flowed up an inch or two higher every other week. You hardly noticed it. And, after all, it flowed out to sea every so often. So what's the problem? Intermittent flood warnings harped on the news. 'Im-Flood' announcements would pinpoint times and places where expected flooding would interrupt your daily round of chores. Easy enough to work around.

And remember this: they told us it was not really happening. They said it was not a problem. They said that global flooding was not true. They said it was a conspiracy started by some rogue Berkeley type. They said that reports of rising waters at sea level were false. Much of the news we got went contrary to what we could see with our own eyes. So we developed mass schizophrenia, of course. This lying leads to a variety of twitching collusion on the part of those of us who listened to, and chose to believe, the lies that were being told to us at the onset of what would later be named The Emperor Tides.

The changing of truth into lies leads to numbness. You begin to doubt your own senses. And you begin to dis-believe what your eyes, your ears, your skin are communicating to your brain and you interpret those sensations as 'lies' and so you start to disbelieve your own eyes, your own hearing, the very sensation of deep water around your ankles. And then you are led into anesthesia where nothing means anything and you don't really feel or see or hear anything that is really happening and so nothing, anymore, is truth. And so, thus hypnotized, anesthetized, and schizophrenic, we took in the reports that denied what we could see with our own eyes and, sooner or later, we just ignored the subtly rising tides. Thus, I was still doing errands in Novato, oblivious to hazard or danger or even to potential drowning. So, I continued shopping at Costco during the periods of time when the waters receded.

Then, unexpectedly, shopping became looting.

Here's how it worked:

I pulled into the Costco parking lot one afternoon. Found a parking place under two feet of flowing water, shut off the car engine, unbuckled my seat belt and, reflexively, swung my left leg out of my car, sloshed rather, up to my shins. The water was dark and stank, badly, of garbage. No problem. I had my galoshes.

Today Costco was having a sale of slightly water-damaged items. Clothing and electronic devices, canned goods with labels washed off. Hand scribbled flyers were stuck onto tree trunks and utility poles around town. Prices slashed. Or maybe that should have read 'splashed.'

Undaunted, ever the optimist at the promise of Sale! Sale!

Sale! I waded up to the doors. With no electricity in those early days of the so-called, 'non-existent floods', Costco was dark. A few customers in their waders were gathering armloads of sodden jammies and bursting soaking sacks of pinto beans.

But you know what?

Nobody was yelling or grabbing.

It was quiet and workmanlike, somewhat business as usual, and not a bit like in your regular disaster movie. It was, in fact, eerily silent without the static buzz of fluorescent lights, without the hum of freezers, without the melodious computer cash registers: gone now, long gone. And, of course, there were surprisingly few shoppers. Just a few bundled outliers sloshing through the dark aisles. People who had not yet gone up hill and who, at this point, still could go up hill, and maybe they would go uphill eventually. Then there was me, determined not to go up hill, but simply to go home after my shopping and tend to my treehouse project.

I gathered up a few label-less and dented cans. Of what, God knew. Was it food? Would it be tainted? Would it kill me? I did not much care. I waded to the front of the store to where the cash registers used to be. Nothing there but octopussing cable branches, cut or torn from their cash registers, long ago looted.

Of course, I suppose I was a looter too. Weren't we all looters at this point? Just quietly going about our business of — and this was the first time I put a word to it — surviving. One reason I believe things were so orderly and silent was that many of the shopper-looters carried weapons. Long serious military weapons. Stubby dark hand guns. No wonder it was quiet and orderly, our looting. I proceeded by keeping my eyes averted and looking only at my feet, mouth shut, grabbed my loot, and got the heck out.

We were already much accustomed to Open Carry by then. Years of Open Carry had inured us to there being anything sinister or dangerous in such a policy. But here's how it really worked, especially as the flood waters rose:

Carry your weapon

In the open

Open fire

Carry on.

Open Carry laws passed without a whimper in all but one state. Hawaii, I think it was. Too bad about that lovely archipelago: glug, glug, now.

When Costco flooded and had its close of business SALE, or Grab-A-Thon, we were silent and orderly when shop-lifting or looting or whatever-the-hell you'd call it. See what I mean?

Before the floods we were already a mess. Civilization — with its orderly nations and states and counties and towns — civilization was already on the decline. My use of the phrase 'on the decline' sounds so prissy compared to the actual reality of our drowning dying civilization. It was breathtaking in savagery. Mind-numbingly fucked, well after the word 'fucked' had lost all possibility of shock in daily vocabulary.

Loaded with my loot, I waded straight out Costco's big doors, mounted my car, would it start? And that was how it started for me. Periodic high tides became, a bit belatedly — stupid me — "The Emperor Flood".

Meanwhile you wonder: Then what?

Look. I'm doing my best here. I'm just an amateur news-caster now. At best an unreliable witness. But here goes:

I knew we were done for when the Severn Bore tides in England got their fifteen minutes of fame. That was months before I started my treehouse project. Regular prophet, I am. Flowing from the Celtic Sea through the Bristol Channel, these tides rolled for eight miles inland into what had been, historically, the bucolic seasonal wetlands running from Sharpness to Gloucester. These tides were not unlike our own seasonal wetlands here on the edges of the San Pablo Bay. High tides here in the San Francisco Bay Area — nicknamed the King Tides — would periodically rise into the seasonal wetlands of Petaluma and Sebastopol. But the Severn Bore tides in Britain were even more formidable. They were strong enough and deep enough and aggressive enough to support dozens of wetsuit-clad surfers and to support their own public relations firm for the creation of the Severn Bore web site.

The tides were gorgeous, really, in their own macabre way, killing adventuresome lads on their surfboards. Surfers were flung off this way and that way onto the muddy and tree-lined embankments. Narrow yellow and orange and snow-white surf boards winged up and over the levies at disturbing odd angles like jet planes going down.

I even witnessed a very surprised swan engulfed in the muddy waves. Watched it on YouTube. I did. People lined up for miles to watch the powerful tides. Larks! It was all picnics and beer and let's go down and see the Severn Bore tides, Maudie. What fun. But to me, watching the strongest of the surfers, not to mention the hapless swan, plow into tree trunks, well, it did not bode well I thought.

One moment they are upright on their surf boards, masters of the water, and next thing you know, they are engulfed in the massive, relentless surges, now flailing with their stick legs and stick arms, tossed haphazard against the black, water-logged trees, broken. These were skilled surfers, seasoned in the monster Atlantic Ocean. And, God knows, the swan was a strong swimmer. Yet, all of them wiped out. Some went missing. Poor sods; poor sodden sods.

The way I saw it, we were doomed. Those accidents caused in me a dawning apprehension: the same thing is going to happen here.

There's going to be another flood I thought. Just like the Severn Bore tides. But worse. Much worse. And these hero-type testosterone-infused morons and wing-ed swimming birds would blithely dip into the new round of flood tides to show that stupid old Darwin was wrong. Yet they would all wipe out in the sheer evil genius of those tides. Those tides. It was enough to make you believe in God.

Or not.

So then. A new flood is coming, I thought. Everybody will die, I thought. Not only those first harbingers of pride and ego and skill, with their swagger and their surf boards and their webbed feet. But every single one of us will die. The fit and the lame. The swimmers and the non-swimmers. Doomed, we all were. That's what I thought back then.

Turns out I'm right. Right? As I said, regular prophet I am. Along with me being a rabbi. That and twenty-five cents!

Let me see: this flood is bound to be larger by far than Noah's old flood. Am I right? Every human being and every animal back then in those biblical times went under in the deluge. Except of course that lucky few in the ark. But anyway, most went under. And how many would that have been? Well let's compare that number, the actual number of victims in Noah's era, with the numbers now, the numbers of our flood victims, caused by this flood, our own Emperor Flood. Whose race is it I ask you? We, by far, will have suffered the greater number of losses. Do the math. And let's not be coy. We, our civilization, has suffered a greater number of deaths. They are all dead. As dead as I will be some day, sooner or later. You think I talk too much about death? So I ask you. What-the-heck else is there to talk about? And who-the-heck else is out there to listen? So criticize if you must. I talk a lot about death because that, dear reader, is the topic I am expert at.

Being human I start to think about God and to sulk. How could He, She or It do this to me? To little innocent me? Sarah Steinway? I ask you. So out of curiosity I turn to the old books. Scripture. Or Torah. Or whatever you call it. I mean. I have no earthly idea what's inside those pages, me secular and all. What's with this God business anyway? And, me being only human, well maybe I hope to find comfort in the old books. Or salvation. Or what-ever-the-heck. Looking for comfort and/or God, I start to read Torah. Can't hurt. Probably won't change anything.

Anyways.

Got to thinking about that first flood. How come Noah's wife got left out of the story? It's all Noah this and Noah that. I bet Mrs. Noah had a thing or two to say.

Midrash One: My Chat with Mrs. Noah

—So how did you feel during the ark period of the flood Mrs. Noah?

—Thank you for asking, dear. Such a good question. People never ask me about all that. It was such a long time ago you know. And dear, dear Noah-y gets all the attention. Not that he doesn't deserve it of course. But, my lands, it was something else, I can tell you.

—Tell me.

—Well the whole thing brings to mind the eternal question, doesn't it? I mean about the poops. Am I right? I mean, what school child in the world never thought about that? Right? Of course, they did. Kids were always afraid to ask: 'But Bubby, what about all the animal shit?' Or, if they tried to ask in a sort of serious way, 'But Mama did all the animals wear diapers?' As far as I see it, diapers or no diapers, either way, it would be work for someone and that someone tended to be me of course, women's work being what it was back then. There was a heap of work below decks, so to speak. Ha! Was that a double entendre? Bet you wouldn't guess I'd have such a penchant for words, for word-play — I who barely merit a mention in all the wordy documentation that exists of that long-ago time. Not to mention the commentary.

—What was Mr. Noah like?

—Noah-y? Well, you know. Men! He never changed a diaper in his life!

—But he built the ark. Isn't that right Mrs. Noah?

—Well there's always one excuse or another. Noah-y was

handy with tools; it is true. But around the ark? Tossed his clothes off the minute he got inside. Never picked up after himself. Wanted meals hot and right on time. I'm not complaining, but it wasn't easy.

Story of life for us females. Do a lot of scut-work and who gets all the publicity? Noah. I actually lived that Mrs. Noah bit. Worked as an advertising copywriter, writing copy for dog food and fast food— that was a whole 'nuther kind of deluge.

See what I mean where thinking about God gets you?

Devolution into self-pity.

I had a pair of lavender suede, wedge-sole, peep-toe shoes: $250 the pair from Joseph Magnin. Brand name. French. And there I sat, up-market chic, pounding away at my typewriter in the creative department. I had advanced in my career, so-called, far enough to actually be able to afford lavender suede shoes at $125 per foot.

Sat around big mahogany conference room tables, knee to knee with men in pinstripes and ties. All innuendo, all the time. Bright eyed and bushy tailed— har har har.

"Nice choice of words. Miz. Steinway." Har, har, har!

Undeterred, I'd toss onto the table my chipper marketing insight. Silence. Throat clearing. Nervous glances. Twenty suited-marketeers harrumphing and squirming. Why didn't one of 'them' think of that?

Then, five, ten minutes later, count the minutes on your Piaget wristwatch, and some MBA kid trainee from research croaks out my idea, repeating it verbatim. And Ah Ha! Now there's the ticket! Bright kid. Good lad. He pants, tongue lolling. Basking in the kudos. Up and coming. Pat, pat on his little crew-cut head. Scratch his ears. Woof!

I got to the point where I'd say, loud and clear, 'What? Is there an echo in here?' You know the scene. Over the years I'd watch my face in the ladies' room mirror. I was turning into one of those women: bright, beaten, boozy. And thus I put the brakes on my meteoric rise. Gave up the ample paychecks. Started wearing the lavender wedgies in the garden.

And I quit.

To paint.

Nowadays, it's all 'Why me, God?' And stuff like that. And then, bargaining:

"Listen God or whoever you are. I, Sarah Steinway, can't just about take any more of this. Are you listening? Is there anybody out there?"

Start to thinking and see where it takes you?

See where thinking about God— He, She or It— gets you? Self-pity. Righteous rage. Useless.

Well, that's it. My personal history of The Emperor Floods is that it started, slow at first. Incoming and outgoing tides alternately flooded and then flowed out to sea again. San Rafael, San Francisco's Embarcadero and farther inland to places like Sacramento and Galt. At first, we made do. Went to work. Went to the bank. Then home again, home again, jiggity-jig. Then it wasn't such a lark any more. It was serious.

News blared all over the channels, throughout the Internet. Lots of talking-head authorities. Lots of congresspersons, senators, city council members, college professors, fringe folk. Even the Leader, 'cap L', got in on the thing, denying it all, of course.

"Impossible! Fake news about lowland flooding! They're always after me for causing their latest disaster! It was my predecessor, dontchya know. Wrong! Sad."

Back then, early days, if they shouted loud enough, it couldn't be true. So much for the statesmen. Person. The Statespersons. Ha!

Then some PR wag made a logo for the 'events' — God forbid you called it a disaster or a catastrophe — and some junior woodchuck copywriter named them 'The Emperor Floods' on account of it being the biggest and worstest floods known to mankind. Personkind. Hell. You couldn't even talk about them without tempers flaring as to grammar and usage. The only person allowed to trample verbal decency was our noble head of state, but really, we were all up shit creek without a paddle.

Then, as whole cities and counties became engulfed in water and panic and anger and fear — then came scapegoating. And litigation began in earnest. Instead of men of good faith gathering in their councils to solve this mess, they gathered in their rage to sue. You can imagine where this led. There was a regular lawsuit bubble.

Scapegoats, the noun plural, and scapegoating, the verb, had their day in court as parties of interest and the parties of standing stepped up to the high platform of the judges. Everyone was suspect. All were sued. And, I ask you, what became of that lovely arcane pursuit, held in ancient wise hearts and preserved in beloved books:

'Justice. Justice shall you pursue.'

Well, we and those noble hopes, were all at sea now.

Sad.

Worse.

Repetition had ruined that little word 'sad' and we were left with nothing to say about how really sad things were.

In another landscape, I could have kept those words alive. But for now, it's all I can do to keep my own body alive. Then the flood waters settled. Stood roiling but no longer rising. Towns, cities, homes — all drowned and destroyed. No more incoming and outgoing tides. Just deep bad water as far as I could see. I mean, from my treehouse all I can see now is water.

Why me?

-III-

... have a good eye. ...

be a good friend ...

be a good neighbor ...

anticipate the future.

Pirke Avot 2:9

Where was I?

Ah, yes. My treehouse. Happy days.

Coincidentally, and providentially as it would turn out, it was around the time of the rising tides that I met my neighbor, Emanuel Epps.

I was seventy-five back then, looking every bit my age. Napping one late afternoon, I awoke with a start, hearing something motorized and loud pull into the driveway across the street. Annoyed and disheveled, I flung open my front door to see who and what had disturbed my introversion.

It's this guy.

Aging hipster with short white hair. A two-wheeled vehicle, no helmet, shit for brains — who rides a motorcycle helmet-less? — yet this guy was simply oozing Bohemian ambience. He was the kind of guy I'd ogle when he passed me on the highway. That's how it once was with me: unseemly old lady assesses asshole on motorcycle.

Feh! I'm only human.

Anyways.

So it's this guy.

He gracefully maneuvers an elaborately decorated Indian®
Motorcycle into a little skid, coming to a halt under an oak tree
next to his driveway. The bike has bulging saddlebags outlined
with serial studs that spell out his initials in an elaborate script:
backwards and forwards facing E's. Emanuel Epps I would soon
learn. He sat astride his machine like a consort, good posture for
an oldish man. I would guess late sixties, legs akimbo, confident,
in control. He switched off, simultaneously swinging his outer
leg up and forward, skimming the handlebars in a balletic arc.
And there he was.

And there we were. Blessed silence.

Ah, men and their machines. God love 'em!

In this moment of silence, I take in the sheer wacky madness
of this man's vehicle. The bike is Candy Color Shamrock Green.
'My Green Machine™' is painted in twenty-first century gothic
script on the gas tank. On the rear bumper is a little metal sign,
shaped like a miniature license plate, and it says: For Emanuel
Labor™ go to www.emanuelabor.org.

I never could resist a pun. And, old as I am now, and old as I
was back then, I still respond to the tug, to the whiff of danger
personified by a wild man and his snarling, roaring beast: the
iconic American motorcycle.

So shoot me!

By this time he senses my aggravated stare and he strides up
my driveway, arm extended. He pumps my hand in forceful and

convivial greeting.

"Epps."

And off we go.

Turns out he's an artist and a builder. Art for the heart. Building for the stomach. As he informs me. If his craftsmanship were to be as deft as his mustache, a downward furled Fu Manchu, then we were in business. I do so love a genuine craftsman. Here he was, builder, artist, owner of tools, and most likely, owner of a mustache comb. Emanuel Epps was just what I needed.

Actually, what I needed, or thought I needed at that time, turned out to be nowheres near what I would come to need pretty soon. When I met Epps, I thought I needed a treehouse. I thought I needed a fanciful treetop retreat, an amusing little garden folly. I could not have known what role my treehouse would play in the years to come. That treehouse would save my life.

And Emanuel Epps?

If you think I fell for Emanuel Epps, you're wrong. Did not! Did not! Did not! Well, maybe a little. But when we met I was already seventy-five. Men like that do not notice women like that. And that is that. And if you are foolish enough to find yourself thinking about a man like Epps, put a barbed wire fence around that thought and walk on. Do not act out. Save those delusions. Nothing but ridicule will come of it, I assure you. So stuff it. Keep it to yourself and do not allow it anywhere near your actual heart. Keep it out of the public eye or you, the old lady with the cats, will become the joke. By seventy-five I knew, full and well, that love can kill you. And then you cry. And there you are.

Am I right?

Women cry because they have lost love.

Weepy old crone.

Where was I?

Ah, yes. Epps.

And so began our folie a deux.

I call him. His cellphone rings a few too many times and I'm ready to leave a message when suddenly he answers:

"Epps!"

Clipped. Abrupt. Noise in the background. Hammers?

"It's me, Sarah Steinway. I've got a house project. You interested?"

"Depends."

"I'm offering cash-money."

"Okay. So?"

Drifting. Tentative. I love this guy!

"So, what I want is a treehouse. Up in the branches of that big Live Oak next to my driveway. The one with the split V trunk?"

"You want a house?"

"Well, maybe not an entire house. A dwelling. A building. A single room with windows and a deck. What I want is …"

"How high up?"

"Well, up in the big branches that, er, branch over my driveway."

"Thirty feet?"

"Something like that."

"How big?"

"What do you mean?"

"Square footage."

"Well, I don't exactly know, Epps. What do you think?"

"How 'bout one hundred square feet?"

"How big is that?"

"Ten by ten. Five by twenty. Two by fifty. You tell me, lady."

He's getting testy.

"Let's say ten by ten."

"And how, pray tell, Mrs. Steinway, do you intend to alight into your proposed Tree McMansion?"

"You tell me, Epps."

"How 'bout a rope ladder?"

"Like a pirate?"

"Wood slats nailed onto the tree trunk?"

"Wouldn't the nails kill the tree?"

"How about stairs, Mrs. S?"

"Stairs? With handrails?"

"Little lady wants handrails! Carved finials perchance?"

I'm not little, and I am not a lady. I take umbrage and raise my voice:

"Handrails. Fine. No finials. How much?"

"It'll cost."

Epps is blowing smoke now. I mean, but literally. I can hear him take a drag on something. Cigarette? Dope? He blows it away from his cellphone.

"Okay. Here's the deal Mrs. Steinway. I'll have to get back to you with a budget. It's not going to be cheap. We'll need a lot of lumber. It's going to be dangerous. I'll want a rig. I'll need to be tethered to the tree when I work up there. Might need assistants. Hampton, Ruggles and Sterns are my guys. It'll be no small investment in steel plates, beams, turnbuckles, flashing, lag bolts, carriage bolts. You name the hardware. Need pulleys and ropes. Augers. Need to rent a truck. Rent table saws, chain saws, chop saws, circular saws, hand saws. Ladders."

Hell. I thought he'd have tools! He's ticking things off on his fingers, I can tell.

"Oh, and we'll need to do tree work before we even get started on the construction. Cabling, pruning, removal. We're not talking cheap, here Mrs. S. Safe is never cheap. Call you back in a coupla days. Thanks for calling Emanuel Labor."

Click.

And that was that. Connection closed. We were on our way.

What I had wanted at that point was a place where I could think. Not that I couldn't have done that inside my house. But it's the aesthetics of the thing. I wanted atmosphere in which to think. I needed detachment. Or so I had thought. No interruptions. No phone. No computer. No doorbell. I needed something at one with nature — if that's not too la-la-woo-woo — in which to think.

By think, I don't mean meditate. Lots of people were meditating in those days. But what I discerned, they weren't meditating as much as they were just thinking and worrying and then snoozing. I can honestly say, what I needed to do was to think. To think it all through, whatever "it" turned out to be.

And what, pray tell, does a woman of seventy-five think about?

I think: this cat will be my last cat.

I think: I don't like to cook anymore.

I think: God, please, let it be quick. Let me just fall to sleep.

I think: I wasted my forties, working as a copywriter, turning mountains of bullshit into molehills of bullshit. I turned entire notebooks of marketing research into clever little 30-second TV commercials. Such a talent I was.

I wanted to have a place where I could think and think and re-think and think again. There would be no provisos, no rules, to govern how I did my thinking. Here's how I wanted my thinking to proceed:

I do not need supervision for my thinking.

I do not need suggestions about what I should or should not think about. I do not need clients or creative directors or editors for my thinking.

I don't care what your opinions are about my thinking.

I do, however, need a treehouse in which to form my thoughts.

I think.

And for that I needed Epps.

Or, and here I go again thinking: I thought I needed Epps.

Or did I just think I needed a treehouse.

Or Epps for that matter?

Wasn't I just making an excuse for making a pass at Epps?

See where thinking gets me?

Two days later I am thinking, sitting at my ordinary desk in my ordinary office and I think: Why do men always, always, interrupt women? I'm pondering this question, wondering, when my cellphone blurts. It's Epps. No greeting.

"Twenty-five grand, give or take."

"Yikes!"

"When do you wanna start, Mrs. S?"

"Hey Epps! You always beat around the bush like this with

clients?"

He is not amused. I change tack.

"So. How long will it take, Epps?"

"Now there's a topic I could write a book. First off there's the necessary tree work. We gotta call Fernando and his guys. Could take a week or so to get them in gear. Then there's hauling and site prep. And I gotta call my guys..."

I interrupt:

"Hampton, Ruggles and Sterns?"

"Good girl. Shows you listen. Gotta get them in order. Rent the truck. Get the lumber, hardware. Oh, and we'll need four safety rigs, not just the one for myself. I gotta think of my guys. As I said, safety doesn't come cheap. I'll keep a running tab on extra expenses."

"You mean on top of the twenty-five K?"

"Then there's the weather. El Nino's coming they say. Could lose a day or two with rain. Between storms the site's gotta dry out. Couple of more days. You don't want to be building a treehouse in the mud. I'd say a good month to six weeks. Give or take."

"So let's review, Epps. It's twenty-five grand, give or take. Plus expenses on a running tab. And it's six weeks, give or take. I give and you take. Is that it, Epps?"

"You getting testy with me ma'am?"

I can feel him smiling. Smirking, more like. Gauntlet flung.

"Come on over, Epps, and I'll give you a down payment and let's get started."

There's a little shuffling sound on his end of the line and then I hear his boots. Minute later, my doorbell. I'm still on the phone. He's on his phone too. He peers in at me through one of my front door side panel windows making that little pen on paper pantomime that you do across the room at a waiter when you want the bill. Wait Person. Sorry. I open the door. We swipe off our phones.

"You want a cup of coffee, Epps?

"You payin'?"

"Put it on my tab, Epps."

I can't help laughing. I didn't blush. Did not! He's so damnably handsome. The Fu Manchu outlines real deep dimples on each side of his jaw.

We sit in the kitchen. It's on the south side of my house and it's late in the afternoon in February so there's a giant slab of sunlight glaring across the tabletop. Epps looks around, appraising:

"Very Frank Lloyd Wright, this house."

"Very. It was built by one of his students from Taliesin West."

"Yeah, I can see that. A real pastiche of Wrightian conceits. Desert rubble pillars. Check. Cantilevered windows. Check. Set on the brow of this hill. A genuine Taliesin setup. Does it leak, Mrs. S?"

"Sieve-like."

"Figures. You always got a problem with your Frank Lloyd Wright derivatives. Those handsome jutting rooflines. Your odd shaped windows. I've rehabbed my fair share of them. Folks can only take so much of the remediation and then they just give up. Pretty soon all they want is a nice dry house. Never mind the architectural gem in a Frank Lloyd Wright. Makes your average tract house look positively tantalizing. But I gotta admit, Frank Lloyd Wright's been good for my business. I've never met a Frank

Lloyd Wright house I didn't come to love for all its lucrative little projects. Especially after it rains. Now your earthquakes, that's a different story. Earthquakes, these houses survive. But two teaspoons of water on a cantilevered window and it's Epps they're calling."

I love this guy. But not like that. Not exactly. But given another time and taking a few decades from my age, and this little tete-a-tete could have taken a turn, if you get my drift. Nothing like a pretty woman staring across a steaming mug of coffee, at a certain type of guy. Sorry. But, as it was, given many, many too many decades, and taking away the pretty woman part, and it's a whole 'nuther thing. I fidget.

"More coffee, Epps?"

"Nah. Gotta go. Gotta get started on this treehouse venture for this lady I know."

He winks, bolts up, bumping the table, catches the edge to steady it. The coffee mugs slosh.

"Gotta go call Fernando about the cabling. See you in a coupla days."

And he's off. Oh well.

"I am my beloved's, and my beloved is mine…"

Or some such: something to that effect.

The Epps team — Hampton, Ruggles and Sterns — were an odd lot I must say.

Eugene Hampton was a twelfth-year Berkeley grad student working on a Ph.D. in The Semantics of Fifteenth Century

Poetry, a project that got pushed farther and farther onto the back burners of his psyche as he took on various long-term construction gigs. He was nimble and taciturn, qualities that aided him in avoiding the quirks of his team-mates.

Ruggles — E. Roger 'Rugged' Ruggles — was a young sixty-six years of age, recently coerced into accepting the dole from Social Security, an indignity he railed against, as a staunch Republican, but which, nonetheless, he watched with a beady eye as the funds dropped into his bank account on each and every second Tuesday of each and every month. 'Don't touch my Social Security!,' he bleated often, and very, very, loudly.

Sterns, Jerry, was a real live redneck survivalist which I discovered the hard way as we set off on our project. There wasn't a conspiracy theory he'd met that he didn't like. As we were getting started, when truckloads of lumber slammed onto my driveway and boxes of metal bolts and braces were being stacked, workmanlike by work-persons, I marveled at the mass of men and materiel that it took to build such a structure. I observed that:

"Hell, if we can send a man to the moon it should be a piece of cake to send him up a tree."

Over to one side I heard Epps cough and could just barely hear him mutter something under his breath:

"Don't go there, Mrs. S."

And, sure enough, Sterns was off and running:

"Do you really believe we sent a man to the moon, Mrs. Steinway? Do you really believe that in that era, that was 1969 remember, that we could have mustered the scientific muscle to actually DO such a trick? Do you? Do you, Mrs. Steinway?

Ma'am?"

I started to respond, but Epps coughed violently with something that sounded like 'HALT!'

"Then you are simply out of your mind. Ma'am. You are simply not getting it straight. Let me tell you how it was. Here's how it was. What it was, was, for your so-called lunar landing, you've got your first rate, top secret, FBI, CIA, NASA top secret operation, not to mention the very highest levels of the US Army, the US Navy and the top masterminds of your thought-control police, it's the media I'm talking about here Mrs. S, on top of your other top secret operatives in all those buildings out there in Bethesda and they were all, ALL I repeat, in it together. Not to mention they put it on TV so we'd all see it happen at the same damn time on so-called Live TV. So-called Live! Back then in 1969? I ask you! Oh, and you know what, Mrs. Steinway? Let's not forget the machinations of your Hollywood Cabal, the Hollywood TV writers and producers, and let us not forget, never forget for a moment, Mrs. Steinway, the power of Post Toasties."

With that he switched his toothpick from one side of his mouth to the other and caught his breath. He was far from done.

"Why do you think, Mrs. Steinway, I drive this Bigfoot Thunderball, five-ton pickup?"

I was baffled:

"Er, why, Jerry?"

"I drive it because some day, and it won't be all that far into the future, that I assure you, THAT mother is gonna save my life. It's going to: Save. My. Life. Do you see, Mrs. Steinway. Do you see what's going on here?"

"What about the Post Toasties, Jerry?"

"The what?"

"You mentioned Post Toasties and the Man on the Moon thing a minute ago."

"Yeah. Oh Yeah. Yes. Don't you see? It's advertising. It's advertising that keeps this whole motherfucker going. It's laughable, really."

He barked a little laugh and out flew the toothpick.

"They've got the whole damn thing wrapped up. You gotta weapon, Mrs. Steinway?"

"Weapon?"

"In the words of the amateur, of the wannabe cowboy, of the homespun home-guard — a gun, Mrs. Steinway. You got a gun?"

"Jerry. No. Of course I don't got a gun. I mean. I don't have one. A gun or weapon or whatever you call it, Jerry."

"Then you have not been listening to me, have you, Mrs. Steinway? It's all going up! When, not IF, the shit hits the fan, you will need to be armed. Armed, yes, and dangerous. If you get my drift. There will be no going back once the shit hits the ol' proverbial. You can say I told you. And don't forget who told you. Me. Jerry Sterns. Because if it's anything for sure, I'll be out of here. Gone. But I will not, I repeat, I will NOT be up shit creek without the proverbial. A paddle, Mrs. Steinway. That's what I'm talking about here. And you, you Mrs. Steinway? You are going to sink or swim and you will need to arm yourself. And never call it a gun. It's a weapon. You understand, Mrs. S? Always utilize proper nomenclature. It's a hard world out there. Mark my words."

He seemed to be winding down. Certainly he was repeating himself. He took a box of toothpicks out of his snap front shirt pocket and sucked in a fresh new toothpick, tucking it neatly into his cheek pocket with just a half inch of the wood protruding from the corner of his lips.

"Damn straight, ma'am."

And off he strode across the worksite, harness untethered, the man too, possibly.

Someday I would thank that man, but first I had to see to the building project. First I had to write the checks. I would have to find myself much farther 'up shit creek without the proverbial' before I would be able to appreciate that guy, that orator of conspiracies, that connoisseur of conspiracies, that guy on my worksite, Jerry Sterns.

As the months floated by, water levels rose during a two-week cycle, no more than a foot or two on the incoming tide, and then it rolled back out to sea, leaving wet, but not impassable, roads. I was still able to continue sloshing out into the so-called seasonal wetlands of the San Pablo Bay to take the long view of my treehouse. Standing now and then in two feet of rapidly flowing water, I could still look across from the top of Day Island to appreciate the progress of my project. It was no problem for your average plastic garden galoshes, although sometimes the mud was so insistent that it sucked one of my boots clean off my foot. Then I'd reach around the top edge of the boot shaft with my white, now muddy, toes, hop around a few hops to wipe my foot off on my pants leg and re-engage the boot. No problem.

What was exhilarating was standing across the estuary on the subtle rise in the landscape that we used to call Day Island, not a real island actually — and to stand over there about a mile from my treehouse and to see it growing up on the topmost branches of my California Live Oak.

At first all I saw from there was the upright beams that stood out in a branching Y shape from the crown of the tree. The enormous tree branches had been cabled to within an inch of life by Fernando and his crew in a process that far exceeded its budget, but that, as Epps pointed out to me, also far exceeded safety requirements and far, far exceeded the allowable stresses for the weight of the eventual treehouse. The tree itself was actually cabled into bedrock. The project, a marvel of over-engineering, would eventually support the floor, the walls, and the roof of the treehouse as it rose well above the canopy of the tree. But Epps, at his most Epps-ian, had this to add:

"We are also building to withstand the very forces of Nature, Mrs. S. What we have with a treehouse is not only the sheer weight of the structure, we have the forces of wind and weather, heat and cold, and rain with its guarantee of hydropower when water streams from rooftop gutters onto the very foundation of the structure. A building is no small marvel of engineering, even a treehouse such as yours, Mrs. Steinway. Thus, there will inevitably be additional stresses, along with the attendant unforeseen cost overages, so you see, Mrs. S, during the building process there is also a process of discovery where overages for architectural reassessment are necessary, yea, and can be lifesaving. This is the evolving process which we refer to as building construction."

Adorable.

He was just adorable, if not an expensive variety of adorableness.

Before the seas rose to their eventual depth, and with

ample time before the worst of The Emperor Tides, I had begun to anticipate my future. As I watched the evidence on YouTube, I began to believe that a killing flood was inevitable. With my treehouse project well under way and not yet under water, I started to worry about my life's work: my paintings. If they, or I, were to attain immortality, I would need to haul them to a higher elevation.

And so, Epps and I drove some of my paintings to a hot dusty garage, one of the outbuildings that stood on land he owned in Placitas, New Mexico, 5,800 feet above sea level. Thus I had acted upon the conceit to preserve 'my oeuvre' in arid desert sanctity. There my paintings stand, even now I suppose, leaning this way and that way, my aspirations, in a garage. But instead of staying uphill myself, I went back down hill.

If Epps was surprised by my request to go back home, he did not say so. He just wheeled the truck around and back we went. Back to the scant eighty feet above sea level where my house resided on the brow of that little hillock, and lately overwhelmed, one tidal inflow at a time, first in, then out, becoming gradually submerged, above the San Pablo Bay seasonal wetlands.

Why would I have done that? There had been warnings. There had been time. If there were enough time — and there most definitely had been — time to build a treehouse, then there would have been time enough for me to have left forever, the Bay Area. But no. It was love. I had to return to my very greatest love. That very greatest, of all my loves, my house. My home.

What? You are asking. What is that about?

More than the skinny boys in my art classes, lo those millions of years ago. More than friends without number. More than ideas, doctrines, principals, philosophies, books, poems, more than my ill-fated affairs with two fascinating passionate loves, a red Fiat and that sexy yellow cheating heart-breaker, my 914 Porsche.

My home.

My home turned out to be my greatest love. A house. An acre. Gardens. Hens.

Looking east, those decades before the flood, standing in front of my Taliesin windows, my eyes became the eyes of my house. We stood there, lovers, intimates. We stood there, together, watching for twenty seasons the inexorability of the slow, and at that time, gentle tides as they lifted, receded, flowed in, swirled out, and rose higher around the roots of the seasonal pink reeds and the silver ankles of the white egrets who inhabited, back then, those seasonal wetlands of the San Pablo Bay.

Taliesin or shining brow. My Taliesin house. It had been the dream of a student architect. His Svengali, Frank Lloyd Wright, had taught him to put the house on the brow of a hill, above the seasonal wetlands of the San Pablo Bay, eighty feet above sea level. The student did this because the Great Man harped on the concept, not on top of the hill where the winds blow fierce, but at the brow, just downhill from the summit, where the house could nestle among the oak trees and peek out each morning at the shining San Pablo Bay.

So I left some of my paintings to live their own lives in the hot desert at the northern escarpment of the Sandia Range, at 5,800 feet in the thin breathless and very dry, I hoped, altitude. And I came home.

How ridiculous, you say. You're uphill of The Emperor Floods. Why go back to sea level?

It was love.

You know how that works.

In walks this guy, ordinary guy, and something snaps.

'I love him, Mama!'

But he's nobody. He's nothing. And his hair is too long. Or too short. Always too 'something' — fill in the blanks — and Mama does not approve.

'But Mother! I love him!'

Only it's not a guy. It was my Taliesin house.

In I walked and, stepping up two silent carpeted steps, I face east in a Great Room, and it was love.

I loved that slanting sunlight through beveled windows. South light. East light. Happy beauty.

And it's all woven into my other love, Daniel. It was our first grown-up house. We were in our thirties when we crossed that threshold of a real living house. We'd wander through our rooms, bumping like pinballs, pinging into this wall and that fireplace and our window seat and our soaking tub, then bumping outside onto this deck and that flower bed and rolling down the hillside, under those oak trees, our trees. And we worked on our love, seeing in our heads a rose garden, a raised vegetable bed, a hen house and, on our butts, we transformed soil and rock and building debris into foot paths and clearings and French drains and a grove of Liquid Amber trees to turn red and golden once a year against the somber green-black of our oak trees.

See what I mean?

And Danny never would have left either.

Flood or no flood.

Ridiculous optimism — the kind you can only summon when you are with the one you love and I had two loves: I loved my Taliesin house and I loved Danny too. Armed with those loves, I know we would both have gone up into the treehouse to sit out The Emperor Flood. Up shit creek without the proverbial. But together. An adventure it would have been. We would have done this together. And, it occurs to me, we would have been the sole survivors, plural.

"Epps, take me home. I want to go back. Home."

And Epps swung the truck around, heading west, and drove me home again.

Soon after our return from New Mexico, I had to graduate from my garden galoshes to fishermen's hip boot waders, courtesy of Jerry Sterns.

"I will tell you this, Mrs. Steinway. Walking in waders is no joke. You must never underestimate even the most shallow of waterways. A tide can be powerful enough, even a very small tide, mark my words, it can sweep you over in a trice. Once you get even a cup of water inside these mothers, the power of the water will fill them up and you will be swept away. And, must I remind you, at first you will not drown, you will panic and your first instinct, to swim or to stand up, will be the wrong one as your waders fill with more hydraulic power than you could ever imagine. You will drown, Mrs. S., but slowly and probably while being carried swiftly out to sea."

"Then I will have you, Jerry Sterns, to blame for my demise?"

"This is no joke, Mrs. S. When the shit hits the fan, and,

believe me, the shit will hit the fan, when it does, it will be sink or swim. Mark my words."

You gotta love a guy like that. Even while fulminating, Jerry was a charmer. His rants and predictions of doom were entertaining and funny, in their way.

I pause here for dramatic emphasis.

Who could have known that he was right? Far, far right, as it was, his view of the world was right on the money.

With the completion of the substructure of my treehouse, the crew was able to quickly install the floor and to raise the wall sections that they had assembled on the ground and then hoisted into place, awkward wings of some giant wooden flying machine. No roof yet, but that would come.

It was time for our topping-out ceremony.

We had planned this event for weeks. On the day of the ceremony, Epps fastened me into one of the harnesses and the guys manned the pulleys that hoisted me aloft, graceful as a netted whale. The stairs and handrails, no finials, were partially complete, halting about ten feet short of the treehouse deck. This was my first trip up to my treehouse: a strange kind of Aliyah, similar to a bat mitzvah I suppose, only I never had one.

As I rose into the tree limbs I marveled at the clear path that the crew had made by trimming branches so that there was a kind of tunnel between the limbs through which they steered me up to the floor of my treehouse. Finishing the stairs was on the calendar for next week. So too, the roof. And of course, these final touches would not come cheap. Stairs and roofs, as Epps reminded me again, do not come cheap.

"A staircase with handrails, no finials. Even without finials, your stairs, Mrs. S, will not come cheap. And let us never forget that a stout waterproof roof is among the most expensive items on any project."

"Weren't those all part of your original estimate, Epps?"

"Of course! But little did we know, at that moment, the many and extenuating circumstances that would add to the final tab."

Of course.

At this point in time, The Emperor Tides, so-called, were rising, gradually creeping uphill day by day, week to week, getting ever closer to our worksite and just a little higher with each new tidal influx.

But today we were topping out. And a little celebratory ceremony was on tap.

Jerry Sterns was soon hoisted up, grasping the rigging with one arm and holding with his other arm an enormous and awkward jutting parcel, a treehouse-warming gift I was to discover. Hampton and Ruggles were next up, each bearing small objects, more gifts.

We stood up there, shoulder to shoulder, standing solid on the floor of the treehouse looking east across the San Pablo Bay waters to what had been Pinole. Except that Pinole was under water now, at least two weeks of every month and what with the disorientation of looking east without seeing a landmass or shoreline in the distance, we could barely take in the enormity of both our predicament and of the significance of my having had this notion in the first place; to build a treehouse. Regular prophet I was.

"Just in the Nicholas of time, Mrs. S."

Epps and I stood shoulder to shoulder on the deck of the treehouse.

"Looks like you're gonna have to move into this sucker and I mean sooner rather than later."

Below us we could hear a swift incoming tide.

Jerry Sterns, ever the prognosticator of doom on our work site, was silent now. Here his most dire of conspiracies was coming true right in front of his face, or should I say, coming right up to his ankles, and he was uncharacteristically quiet. It was actually coming to pass. Shit was hitting the fan.

But Epps was first to see the future of my treehouse. Be careful what you wish for. All I had wanted was a charming little treehouse. A garden folly. Only now it felt like a portent, my wishing for this treehouse. Now it would be the world's folly I would need to assuage.

Hampton spoke next. Scanning his binoculars across to the east and then farther south, it was water, water, everywhere. He did a little tooth sucking thing:

"There goes Berkeley. I guess that puts the kibosh on my Ph.D."

Ruggles was quietly steaming, holding a little pine branch he'd hacked off for our topping-out festivities. He had a way of breathing in through his nose and expelling it, long and tuneful, with a little throat action, a repressed humming sound which I learned meant that, in a minute or two, he'd start holding forth. And that he did:

"Damned freeloaders! Always want something for nothing.

And look where it got us. I guess that puts the kibosh on my Social Security payments."

And with that he hoisted the pine bough overhead, whacking it into place with a single swing of his hammer. It made a memorable splitting sound as a very long nail drove home through the tender little branch. Ouch!

I had bundled into a blanket a loaf of bread, some canned olives, bottled jams, a few cans of beans, and five bottles of Chateau Lafitte Rothschild. With imminent drowning and pending doom, what's the point in saving one's most treasured wine offerings? I ask you. Topping out would be held in style.

Suddenly Jerry switched on. He seemed pleased with himself. After years of preparation and hectoring to the drunk or the disinterested, he had been proven correct:

"See! I told you!"

So, he was positively kittenish in his glee, flirtatious and giggling with me, bon vivant and comradely with the men. Epps was poking at the enormous blanket-shrouded parcel Jerry had lugged up for the party.

"All right, Sterns. What's in this thing?"

"I am glad you ask, my man. And happy to elucidate."

My man? Elucidate? Certainly not typical Sterns-isms. Now he was chummy and bright-eyed.

"What I have here is a treehouse-warming gift for the illustrious and charming and beautiful Mrs. Sarah Steinway."

He bowed at the waist in my direction.

"The wise, the gentle, the perspicacious Mrs. S."

That was a bit thick.

"What I have here is a Number "A-One" SHTF Operational

Life Kit, courtesy of the Benjamin A. Dempsey & Company LLP of Akron, Ohio. One of a kind, as all such kits are, assembled to customer specifications. And I, in proxy for you, Mrs. S., have assembled one heck-of-a-kick-ass Life Kit for you."

I knew better than to ask what SHTF meant. If you, dear reader, do not know what that stands for by now, you are sadly out of touch with the vernacular. Jerry placed the parcel on the floor next to me, folded his arms around his chest to rein in his enthusiasm, vigorously nodding in my direction:

"Go ahead Mrs. Steinway. Open her. Open her!"

I started pawing at the parcel which was very heavy and very awkward, a lumpy offering from this man, this kid really, acting like he'd just handed a present to a grown-up. He was visibly proud of himself. Wrapped in a Bekins moving blanket, Jerry's gift was secured with moving straps wound this way and that. I tugged at my customized Life Kit, eventually exposing the following items:

A CB radio with a hand crank and a solar power array; two large pails, which would eventually be for "incoming" and "outgoing" Jerry informed me, but currently containing: water purification tablets, desalinization tablets, first aid kits with bandages, creams, tweezers, pain killers, antacids, recreational drugs; and one ominous bottle labeled "for extreme emergencies." Then there were boots, waders, rubber clogs, daylight and night-vision binoculars, a Zippo Emergency Fire Starter, ponchos, sweaters, caps, hats, sun goggles with straps, wool scarves, jeans, canvas shorts, tank tops, water bottles, rechargeable flashlights, a machete, an entrenching tool, a compass, a lasso of reflective rope, a First Priority Knife, and, two Every

Hunter's Friends, which were floppy man-sized suits made to look like trees.

"Jerry! What-the-heck are these for?"

He leaped over to me, shaking out one of the folded suits, and held it up full length, against his body. Then he slipped the twiggy thing over his head, becoming completely engulfed in it. His voice was muffled under the weight of the fake leaves and mosses:

"A disguise, dontchya see, Mrs. S.? A hunter's best friend. You never know, I repeat, you never do know when you will need to disguise yourself as innocent flora in a violent world. Trust me. You will thank me some day for these suits. Except for one thing, Mrs. S. I won't be here to say, 'you're welcome.' I will be long gone I assure you of that. But I will have done my level best to outfit you with the essentials to survive in an unsurvivable world context. If you follow what I'm saying."

Unblinking, we all just stared at him. Nodding vigorously, he shifted his toothpick in his mouth somewhere under the suit and spat. The toothpick flew out forcefully from beneath the limbs of his Every Hunter's Friend. What are you going to say to a gift like that?

Then, lastly, Jerry presented me with a pistol and a .12 gauge, pump-action shotgun. There was a small flourish as Jerry stood up, hand to heart, removing the top portion of the Hunter's Friend suit and proclaiming, somewhat grandly:

"Now that you, Mrs. Sarah Steinway, have successfully passed the Jerry Sterns Tactical Training with Firearms Course, you will be highly equipped, if not completely qualified, to protect yourself from a fiendish assortment, a veritable plague, of bad guys. While not having become the marksman, er, marksperson, that we might have hoped for, you have shown courage and focus for self-preservation of yourself, um, on the field of battle. Now that the Shit is truly hitting the fan, I can attest that you are prepared to hold your own. My congratulations, Mrs. Steinway."

It was true. Jerry had trained me, somewhat successfully, to engage a weapon in self-protection.

He stumped over to me, grabbed my hand in a firm and vigorous handshake, and I was set. I guess.

"And what's with these, Jerry?"

I had started going through the piles of waterproof boxes, opening each one and finding more and more useful objects for my survival kit. One box, quite heavy, was stuffed with cartons of cigarettes and dozens of hip flasks of cheap brown liquor.

"That, Mrs. S, is your stash. It's gold out there where money no longer carries any currency, er, if you see what I mean. You gotta buy something, or some-ONE..." He drifted off, he winked at me significantly:

"If you get my gist."

I nodded.

"You simply offer a couple of packs of ciggies and a bottle of booze, Mrs. S., and you've got yourself a deal. These commodities are as valuable to you as bullets. Might just save your life."

I just stared at him. Strange, crazy-assed, Jerry Sterns. One day I would owe him my life.

Then it was Hampton who stepped up with his gift: a black case with a handle and a trash bag filled with odds and ends. It was an Underwood Typewriter, 1950s vintage, a dozen spare typewriter ribbons, twelve reams of paper, twelve boxes of Dixon Ticonderoga pencils, and a manual pencil sharpener shaped like a nostril.

"For you, Mrs. Steinway. What's left of my Ph.D. Use it in good health."

His gifts presented, Eugene Hampton sat down to dine on beans, olives, and bread, washing it down with a swig of excellent wine.

"Where are you planning to go, Eugene?"

"Don't know, Mrs. Steinway. Haven't decided. Maybe..."

Indecisive as usual, he chewed and stared across the bay.

"Maybe ...I don't know. I just ..."

Then Ruggles coughed and stepped forward to present me with his gift. Wrapped in an old Grateful Dead tee-shirt was a well-thumbed paperback copy of the U.S. Constitution.

"No matter how life plays out, Mrs. Steinway, never underestimate how you will draw comfort from the words of our Founding Fathers. And no matter what the circumstances, you will find in this slim volume a guideline to, and the seeds of, your future well-being. Mark well the passages about freedom of speech, equality, and for literal, and I do mean literal, sustenance, check out the section on the Second Amendment about the right to bear arms. This covenant was not meant to be taken lightly, nor was it to be misinterpreted by slack jawed, left-wing leeches mooching off the fat of the land. Stand firm, Mrs. Steinway, and you will always have this document to stand at your side."

It would be much later that I would discover what Ruggles was going on about.

Speech concluded, Ruggles performed a crisp right face,

turning to Epps with the following fare-thee-well:

"It has been an honor and a pleasure to work for a man such as yourself Emanuel Epps. In this day and age of people with their hands outstretched for the free ride, er, it was a joy to toil alongside one who values a day's work for a day's pay. Which, speaking of which, I extend my hand to you for my just rewards."

Epps had already reached into his hip pocket producing a fat envelope which he presented to Ruggles with a handshake, a manly embrace, and a little, somewhat-botched, military salute.

"You taking off then, Rug?"

"You bet I'm taking off, Epps. I am going east soon as the tide goes out tonight. East into the sunrise as the sun rises on the morrow. It's been a pleasure, sir."

And with that, Ruggles was off, swinging down the branches, thumping down the unfinished stairs, and off into the evening. Ruggles. A man alone with his Social Security number and his last day's pay. Except there was nowheres to spend that cash and certainly no need for that nine-digit identifier in this new era of nothing but deep black water.

Jerry was next up and Epps reenacted the payroll officer pantomime, finishing with a traditional manly handshake.

"I'm out of here, too."

"Okay, Jerry. Travel well."

Jingling his truck keys in his pocket he said his fare-the-well:

"Tide's about low enough for driving. I'm off then."

And that was it. Jerry Sterns, a one-man band for catastrophic thinking, clambered down the tree, banged shut his driver-side door, roared up the engine, and he was gone.

Epps turned to me:

"Well Mrs. S. You up for finishing what we've started?"

"I'm up."

"What about you Hampton? You game?"

"I don't know, Epps. On the one hand: what-the-heck else I got to do? On the other: I gotta get up to dry land. My folks live in Albuquerque. Not much water there. Lots of refugees I guess."

"This is yes? Or this is no, Eugene?"

"I guess, no, then, Epps."

Eugene Hampton, decisive as a windmill in a tornado, stood up, wiped his mouth on his sleeve, gave me a strange embarrassed hug, shook Epps's hand, and wobbled down and out and off into the sunset. Uncertain as always, Eugene Hampton disappeared from our lives. So too, Ruggles and Sterns. Would it be forever? We assumed it to be so.

"So, it's you and me, Sarah?"

"Okay. Yes. Just you and me, Epps."

And so, we — Hampton-less and Ruggles-less and Sterns-less — there we were, just us two.

We could have fled, you say?

Are you kidding? And stifle the momentum of our quixotic project? The Don himself always knew his project was doomed. And did he quit? No. He rode on. He beat on against the enemy windmills.

Nope. Epps and I did not quit and softly ride uphill into the credits, long shot, pull back, happy lovers, swell of music, ah, what a pretty movie!

Nope.

We regrouped.

"Well, Mrs. S, it's a cinch we can't get any more building

supplies. Bay Area home centers are well under five feet most days now. And that's permanent, not just at high tide. Need to improvise. What we have here is opportunity!"

This was Epps at his most Epps-ian.

He thunks a forearm around my shoulder as we stand in the unfinished treehouse looking up at the dark, full canopy of my California Live Oak.

"You game Mrs. S?"

"Game."

Oh, and while you're at it, kiss me you madman. Take me into uncharted waters you tritest of similes, a man with a motorcycle. It was the Fu Manchu mustache that unhinged me. I sat there, silent, listening to my muddled thoughts and instead I said:

"So then. What's next, Epps?"

"You, dear girl, are going to have to toughen up and start pulling your own weight. No more leisurely hikes out to Day Island to look wistfully back at what money can buy. Abso-damn-lutely, no! No more of that. Now you will have to sing for your supper. In other words, work your way to the finish line on this little venture. And it won't be easy, I assure you that."

I wanted to quip that it wouldn't be cheap either but decided to hold the thought.

"What we need to do is improvise. In the usual course of a building like yours, we would at this point put the roof on. Then, dry and safe from the elements, we'd install insulation on walls and ceiling and then over that we would staple on your drywall, give it a swipe or two of wall texturization, paint it for aesthetical reasons. Well, none of that is possible now. So: what to do, what to do?"

He removed his forearm from my shoulders, took out a cigarette, put it back, took off his cap, put it back, and wandered around my one hundred square feet of floor, deep in conversation with himself — said conversation punctuated with a lot of what-ifs and on-the-other-hands, interspersed with exclamations of "Nah!"

Then there was a very long silence while Epps withdrew another cigarette and put it back. Took off his cap and swiped a hand through his hair. Walked a few paces more. Spat overboard.

"You got any dry blankets Mrs. S?"

I did, in fact, have some still-dry blankets. At this point my tri-level Frank Lloyd Wright derivative was only flooded on the bottom floor, downhill from the rest of the house. Upstairs, where kitchen and master suite were, it was still dry, although the whole place stank of god-knows-what odors of the flood. Mildew seems a prissy little word to describe the smells that flowed in and out with the tides. There was a lot of dead material in that water. It was early days, and human and other animal remains sloshed back and forth with the tides. More about that later. For the time being, yes, I did still have some dry-ish blankets and a couple of rolled-up rugs that might work.

"What's your thinking Epps?"

"Insulation."

"Just blankets?"

"Actually, not. Here's the deal. We staple blankets and rugs to the walls. Then line them with bookshelves and books. As many books as you can stand to lug up those stairs, Mrs. Steinway. As many as you can possibly, or impossibly, lug up here. But I'm getting ahead of myself here. First we do the roof."

We looked up at the roofless little structure, into the branches of my tree.

"So, Sarah!"

"Yes, Epps."

"You're an artist. Right?"

"You have blown my cover, Epps. Yes. In a manner of speaking. I paint. You know this about me already."

"And these pictures are your oeuvre?"

"Don't mock, Epps. It's unkind."

"No, no. You misunderstand me. I love and admire your paintings. Albeit they are weird. And, as we both know, I am guardian of a fair number of your masterpieces at my home in New Mexico. I am ever the fan of your surrealistic imagery. I myself tap into the deepest interstices of my brain to grasp inspirational and surrealistic grist for my own creative mill. But now, at this juncture, I see in your paintings, the solution to our latest conundrum."

Adorable. He was just adorable.

"You mean a cheap substitute for actual roofing material, Epps?"

"Not exactly. In fact, using your paintings as roofing material will actually cost more than I had originally estimated for the project. That's because I will need to apply more engineering skill — plus the time it takes to apply it — to roofing solutions — well, you can see for yourself that this kind of work requires more skill and more time on the jobsite than your average common roof. Not to worry. It'll go on your overages. No problem."

At this point money was, yes, quite a problem. Everything

was down. No more going down to the grocery store and sticking your debit card into a handy money machine. It was all of it — grocery store, money machine, credit, debt, banks, foodstuffs, parking lot, well you see — it was all under water. Frankly, I was not very worried about my project overages at this point. I would worry about those later, said Scarlett O'Hara.

And thus, the birth of my canvas roof was midwifed by Emanuel Epps.

"Here's the deal Mrs. S. Your canvas paintings, many of which measure, say seven feet by five feet, are a useful size for a gabled roof. And the very substance with which you paint, acrylic medium, is itself waterproof. And the very acrylic varnish that you apply to each finished painting creates yet another layer of waterproofing. And voila! Bob's yer uncle! A sturdy and waterproof — am I repeating myself? — a sturdy and waterproof, built-to-last, treehouse roof. This is all about Taliesin roofs, Sarah."

"What do you mean, Epps?"

"So Sarah: Back when Frank Lloyd Wright conceived of his project in the Arizona desert, he viewed the complex as a kind of camp. The camp was to be built on the raw desert landscape. The sand, and stones, and even the hot and dry air, would be the inspiration for the architecture. Mr. Wright decided to assemble his acolytes and camp out year-round on the desert floor, and everyone could live in tents. Some tents!

"Initially, the project took shape with a huge open space, covered in flapping canvas and with windowless windows and more flapping canvas for shades which opened onto the desert landscape. This tent-like place allowed the acolytes to embody the desert as they developed what was to become a new kind of architecture."

Gaining momentum with his mansplaining, Epps continued:

"But within the folds of the monomaniacal and terrifying Frank Lloyd Wright brain, new ideas kept popping up, new extensions for the buildings, new experiments to wage in his constant battle to keep up with his own overwhelming creativity. The project in the desert, Sarah, now called Taliesin West, grew from temporary encampment to national landmark. And it was there that Mr. Wright considered a new kind of roof. As the project evolved so too did the sophistication of the roofs, especially the roof that covered the enormous drafting room. With a stroke of genius (and were not all of Mr. Wright's ideas stroked by genius?) the canvas roof was invented. Canvas fabric was stretched over wooden frames creating panels that were installed on beams above the drafting tables. Outside, the panels formed the roof. Inside, the panels formed the ceiling. The stretched white canvas panels dispersed a golden, even, and shadowless illumination throughout the massive work room. There was sunlight without overbearing heat or glare. Some of the panels became sliding doors, to open or to close as the building got hotter or colder. The moveable panels made for a kind of air conditioning. Canvas panels stretched on wood frames were well suited to the desert."

Epps stopped abruptly.

He had been gesturing with a wing-like beating of his arms overhead as he embodied for me the canvas roofing over our heads. In slow motion, he lowered his arms. He flicked his vision to the east, fastening on a distant vague chop in the outgoing waters.

He loved me.

Verbal wild goose chase.

Funny way to say it.

But I knew.

He knew it too.

"Well, Sarah. Roofing we need. Canvas we have."

"Yeah."

"Believe me, Sarah. I've rehabbed enough of these Frank Lloyd Wright derivatives to know a thing or two about the Great Man's madness."

He paused again: stuck.

"Most of which did not hold water. Ha! But some of which might solve the problem we have at hand: how to put a roof on a treehouse with no building materials."

It was love, I tell you.

But I would not, no never, ever let him know that I knew. Do not act out. Or you, the old lady with the cats, will end up in tears.

In the days that followed, Epps hastily finished the stairway and handrails: no finials. Then he got busy with the roof. As he worked overhead, I started hauling my books. I stacked and toted by the armload books, and books, and more books until I could not breathe. We would need enough books to line all the interior walls of my treehouse. Approximately four hundred square feet of books. Give or take. And it was killing me to drag them up those stairs. But you know what? After a few dozen trips up my stairs, I started to get strong. I mean my arms, my calves, my lungs. I started to feel muscular, athletic even. It was a form of physicality I was not used to, and I loved it. Little did I realize how much this workout would serve me in the months — and years as it turned out — to come. If I hadn't been seventy-five, I would have looked like Wonder Woman. Well, I was a wonder of sorts: stringy, boney, but very very strong after all this work. Epps. My own personal trainer. Did he know what he was doing? I would wonder about that later.

At night, after the roof and interior work, Epps and I slept together on the floor of the treehouse. It's not what you're thinking. We were so utterly exhausted, so thumped; we would just flop down to die. As good as. Our sleeping was so sound, so stunned, that we would barely move all night long. Then, as the morning sun inched in my front door, we'd wake and sit up and for a few sleep-drugged silent moments we would think. I think.

And hadn't that been what I had originally wanted from my treehouse? A place to think? Well now the thinking time was here and the treehouse held fast for all the thinking in the world. But it was not the kind of wispy woo-woo thinking I might have envisioned back then. This was serious. This was life and death.

"We're all going down, Sarah."

"Not necessarily."

"Yes. Necessarily."

"So? What? What are you saying, Epps?"

"Well, Sarah Steinway as in piano, what if we do the corn-ball thing. Choose life. L'chaim! Like the rabbis told us."

"Told us?"

"Yeah. Us. What do you think kind of name Epps is? It's Epstein, don't ya know?"

"What-the-heck kind of name is 'Dontcha-No'?"

"You, Mrs. Steinway, are a Wise Acre. In addition to being a piano."

Adorable. He was absolutely adorable.

"Seriously, Sarah. We are all going down. Staying here in this treehouse, you'll never live to tell it."

"What, you're telling me to choose life or some such? Off into the sunset with you? Stop. Just stop it. And as for your "choose life" — as far as I can tell, we did not choose life. It chose us. We just suddenly popped out into the world without anybody asking beforehand if we even wanted a life. It was never about choosing. So, as it stands, if you are alive you, already by default, are chosen for death. So, what's the point of fleeing so-called death? It's inevitable whether or not you choose, as if choice were a choice, whether or not you choose life."

"Sarah! You're a rabbi!"

He grabs me and starts to wrestle, then to tickle my ribs and waist, and I'm rolling around on the floor screaming, giggling, undignified, legs akimbo, hair askew. Not behavior fit for a lady, I might add.

"Stop it Epps. Stop it I tell you!"

And he did. He drew back. I sat up. We both turned our heads toward the sunrise. He jumped up, still lithe and limber, and in three strides was out the front door and across the deck.

"That reminds me, Sarah. Got another treehouse-warming gift."

He starts pulling on a rope that's draped, heavy and swaying slightly, over the rail. Attached to this rope, strung part way up from the ground already, are two half wine barrels filled with dirt. He's made an awkward loose rope net to hoist these objects and pulls them up and over, thumping, onto my deck.

"Fruit of the vine. And veggies."

In one is planted a twig of grapevine. The other lies dormant with god-knows-what. Regular garden of Eden.

"It's just, we could still get out of this mess, Sarah. Together."

"Yeah. Okay, Epps. I know. I know. It's just that I am staying."

And now develops a melancholy little fare-thee-well, launched with a gentle inhale, a retention in the lungs, and a slow blue exhale.

His fingertip and thumb proffered to me a flat, inflamed little scroll that was rolled around something. From Epps, it was an offering. A wisp of blue smoke trailed upward from its lighted point, orange with heat.

I took it.

Delicately, as if handling an insect that I hoped to save by flinging overboard, I took the little scrolled item, breathed in, then out, then in again, and blew the burnt offering into the afternoon air.

Nice.

This was not in answer to anything that was going on down there, in the waters beneath my treehouse.

House of tree.

Tree with house.

Mine.

An outgoing tide of black water swirled around the big trunk of my oak tree. Incoming, this tide would embrace my tree. During the waning of the moon, there was bare muddy ground beneath my treehouse. Passable still, but there was nowhere to go nowadays.

People had fled. Going uphill. Panic had ensued of course. On my CB radio, we heard about gunshots on the roadways between San Francisco and Albuquerque. Miles of traffic jammed up going east and vehicles stalled in place. People running up and down the highway, some having given up their cars altogether and set out to walking, further complicating the impassable jam-ups. And all the loving-kindness in what was left of our little world was gone too, replaced by rage and killing even. Roving bands of teenagers. So said the CB radio. Why always teenagers? Plenty of adults were roving. In bands. Fires and explosions blew up as stranded autos were set ablaze. Why? Just for the spectacle of it?

Now we were falling. Civilization is that fragile.

Really, civilization — with its four letters 'i' — civilization, the word, contains too many 'I's and not a single 'We'. If you get my drift.

Ha. Ha. Funny that.

With those darkling thoughts in my mind, and as if from a distance, I could hear us laughing. First as if it were not me or Epps, sources of the laughter. Then as, oh yes, that's us laughing. The conclusion was that we were, indeed, the laughers, and that conclusion was so wonderfully and hysterically funny, a relief actually, and as funny a joke as any joke we had ever heard. Ever! Laughing and laughing.

Enough!

And we stopped laughing.

Enough, already!

And I sat silent, tailor style, examining my fingerprints.

And Epps sat silent, tailor style, examining his palm.

"Solipsistic," I said.

He moved his gaze rapidly, and from his hand, in a great arcing swoosh, shot a luminous con trail. His neck, his hair, his nose, were all illuminated by a sparkling comet's tail, in motion, right there, sitting on the floor of my little treehouse. Beautiful.

"Narcissistic," he said.

"Self-absorbed," I said.

"Selfish," he said.

"Self-centered," I said.

"Stuck up," he said.

"Egoistic," I said.

"Egomaniacal," he said.

"Egoistical," I said.

Then I said, all in one breath,

"Overweening, pompous, smug, vain, vainglorious, ridiculous."

Another bout of laughing, hiccoughing, and then, after, a cough, and I said,

"Survivor."

And Epps said,

"Lone."

"Now see what you've done, Epps. I'm crying."

"Foolish," he said.

"Stupid. Stupid," I said.

"We could have been. Sarah."

"We could have been companionable, Epps."

"Are you listening, Sarah?"

"You have been a good neighbor, Epps."

"I'm leaving, you know, Sarah."

"I know."

"I'm driving north then east. See if I can avoid this shit. Heading for Montana or somewheres uphill."

"To do what?"

"Who knows! Maybe I'll find another Frank Lloyd Wright pastiche to waterproof. Or build an ark. I'll improvise."

"Well, I'm staying, Epps. If this place was good enough for my little student of Frank Lloyd Wright, then it's good enough for me. And besides, I want my money's worth for this damn treehouse. I gotta amortize this folly of a treehouse to pennies a day. That will take time, Epps. Especially with the overages."

"Sarah. Stop it. You'll be okay?"

"Okay. Yeah. Very okay."

He pulled out of his jacket pocket the Emmanuel Epps, LLP letterhead entitled: Expenses Steinway Treehouse. Much rumpled and showing signs of having been dropped into the water, the document was a bit the worse for wear. He handed it over to me.

"If we meet again, Mrs. S, use these papers as proof of who you are."

"Oh Epps!"

I whacked him with the papers.

He thumped the door frame of the treehouse, shaking his head.

"Almost forgot."

He pulled a cigarette pack out of his shirt pocket and tapped it on his knuckles. Out came something; a cigarette I supposed. With a swift move, he flipped a little hand hammer out of his side belt-loop and whacked a couple of times at the doorframe.

"And this sucker. Won't leak no matter what. Tell 'em Epps built it. Built it to last!"

He dusted off his jeans and stomped dry mud off his work boots. Another appreciative thump on the doorframe and he was on his way. He strode across my treehouse front deck and took the stairs two at a time down, jumping the last four steps onto the ground. He shouted up to me:

"Stairs with handrails. No finials!"

And he was off.

It was almost sunset. The tide was outgoing. Going. Going. Gone. There would be a few inches of water covering Highway 37 heading west. Epps could manage that easily on the bike. Then he would turn north onto 101.

I fumbled to stand up. Dashed, well, staggered out onto my deck. Then, using the ladder that Epps had insisted upon, another of those overages, I clambered onto my treehouse roof. From there I could see Highway 37, straight and shining under the shallow water. The sun was setting, illuminating the immersed highway, making it into a dazzling golden arrow, speeding straight west.

He was down there. Tiny from the vantage point of my roof, but I could discern, maybe only in my memory's imagination, his straight spine, legs akimbo, astride that ridiculous Green Machine, saddlebags bulging with tools and canned beans. A great wing-ed spray of water rose from the wheels of his bike as they spun in the shallows and created a spectacular V-shaped arc, on the point of which sat Epps. The man and the water bedazzled in the setting sun. Epps had made his grand exit. And don't tell me he didn't know, full and well, how this would look and how I would be able, later, to conjure it up in my imagination.

Forever.

Fool: me more than he.

I clambered back down onto my deck. A little brass object caught my eye. Upper right door frame. Tipping forward. A mezuzah.

Overweening.

Pompous.

Smug.

Vain.

Vainglorious.

Ridiculous man.

-IV-
If I am not for myself,
who will be for me?
. . . if I am for myself alone,
then what am I?
Pirke Avot 1:14

AND SO, MY LIFE ALONE BEGAN.

For a moment after the exit of Epps, I just sat up there on my catwalk, squinting into the west. Nobody was on the highway now. With the tide receding, it would have been possible to drive any vehicle with a high axel. But, the truth of it was, there was nobody around anymore. At the high-water mark, all of Marin County was under water by five feet or more. Only fools like us, like me, were out on a limb, leftovers from some brave and idiotic sense of immortality. Did I actually believe I could survive this thing?

To tell the truth, I did not think one thing or another. Except to finish my treehouse. That, I had wanted to do. As if I were a corporate project manager, I had set a deadline and, deluded or not, I was sticking to it. And we did complete the task. On time, if not on budget.

I climbed down the ladder and thumped onto my deck.

Home.

This would be my first night sleeping here alone.

I ducked inside and rolled down the canvas door which Epps had installed, in lieu of an actual door, on the top of the door-frame like an old-fashioned roller shade. What? Was I afraid someone would spy me taking off my clothes? Habit. It was just a stupid habit. As the days went by, I was able to just leave the canvas flaps rolled up on my door and windows and my reflex to undress in private bit the dust like every other reflexive habit of civilization. 'Night, dear. Sleep tight.' Things like that.

I rolled out my futon and a blanket and lay on my side facing the darkening east. There would be no town lights across the bay. Pinole was under water, long gone.

Now I lay me down to sleep.

The treehouse was tight. On this first night alone, lone survivor, I could really appreciate its steadfastness. I could just lie here and listen.

Fernando and his crew had made a monumental job of the cabling. Not only had they bound the upper limbs of my oak tree with a series of interlacing connections that formed a jungle gym of triangles above the treehouse, but they had actually anchored the tree to bedrock. The braided and twisted steel cables went down at pyramid angles into the earth around the dripline of the tree's canopy. It seemed, at the time, to be massive over-think, a folly of engineering that I would pay enormous overages on. But as I lay there on that first lone night, I could appreciate its utility. Now that I was alone, my attention was focused on this engineering marvel.

The tree groaned with the hydraulic force of the now-incoming tide. I heard loud snaps of wood under pressure and softer squeaks like old wood floorboards under foot. The massive upper limbs of the oak tree played a wooden tune against the shore breezes, and the cabling harped a sonorous song in a minor key. Fog rolled in around the leaves and I heard them dripping.

The tree embraced me. Lying on my futon I could put my ear against the floorboards and listen to it. My ear, like a stethoscope, picked up my tree's beating heart, little pops of wood in expansion and contraction, like breath, in and out, in and out. And I fell to sleep and dreamed I was walking in high heel shoes on a glass sidewalk.

Life, alone, for me, sole, began with dreaming.

Waking, I realize that though my treehouse roof is made out of my paintings, nobody will ever see them. Well, probably nobody. If there had been a remnant of Day Island, I might have been able to wade out there and, looking back, to see my own paintings displayed like advertising billboards along a highway, clear and bright and garish. Advertising what, exactly? Well, maybe simply, just that there is a roof on a treehouse out there and the roof is made of pictures.

'Look, Mom. A treehouse with a roof of pictures.'

I rolled onto my back to look at my paintings overhead. Epps had made them into ceilings as well as roofs. And the bright colors and bold figures catch the slanting sunlight as it sweeps, rising on the new day, shining on first one picture and then another. Reflected sunlight casts about and illuminates the whole room like flickering flames from a fireplace at nighttime, warming but never burning. My grape vine blows a bit in the breeze outside, its leaves form wavering shadows that look like continents on my pictures. Funny. Continents. Now there aren't any. It's just me.

At the fluttering of the grape leaves, I cannot help but remember just one last image of Epps.

He had hoisted onto my deck those two half wine barrels. With a little Vana White flourish he announced:

"Ta Dah!"

He was so amused with himself and continued:

"White seedless grapes, Sarah."

He gestures to the first barrel with its little grape vine. Then he turns to the other barrel:

"And this barrel, Sarah, is for your seeds."

"Seeds? What seeds, Epps?"

"Sarah! I can see you have not yet opened your copy of the U.S. Constitution. You should check it out sometime soon, Sarah. You may be surprised at what you find therein."

Puzzled, I reached for the copy of the Constitution that Ruggles had given me. Tucked inside the section about a well-regulated militia was an envelope. I shook out the contents — seeds! — zucchini, pole beans, and was that chard?

Ruggles!

"Never underestimate, Mrs. Steinway, how you will draw comfort from the words of our Founding Fathers. You will discover in this slim volume the very seeds of your sustenance."

Very good, Ruggles.

Very clever.

I was ready.

So off to work I go. High ho. High ho.

Oh yes. That old work ethic thing does not die with the last gasps of civilization. And, in fact, my opinion is that work, as such, saves lives; saved mine, I would discover later.

And so, morning one, I must simply get up, get started. God help me.

Or not.

You could go crazy. And so here I go.

All those human beings and their aspirations, drowned, then pushed across waterlogged lowlands into the San Pablo Bay and south to what used to be the gorgeous San Francisco Bay and out to sea. Except that now it was all sea, all ocean, all water, and it was all clogged with refuse: buildings, automobiles, plastic objects both mundane and extraordinary, a prosthetic foot, a dog chew toy shaped like a squirrel, a ballet shoe, a belt, a condom, hell, condoms in their millions. A set of measuring cups, lashed together, still, with that little round metal thingy. Empty water bottles. A rake. A checkbook cover, a pen, a computer keyboard, a stethoscope, and this discovery: plastic items that would have been too heavy to float, sat atop rafts of other plastic things that had bound themselves together.

And how had all this plastic refuse bound itself together?

It was embraced, as it floated, by dismembered human limbs, rotting, now stinking, forming a grisly primitive glue that created oozing and stinking architecture.

One thing about plastic, it does not stink.

It was the human detritus that stank.

Who could have imagined that a secondary character in a first-rate movie "The Graduate" would have been the prophet of all this. Who could have imagined that the neighborly neighbor, Mr. McGuire, when he was giving Benjamin, a recent college graduate, career advice — who could have imagined how truly prescient that advice would turn out to be.

"Plastics Benjamin! 'Nuf said!"

Who could have imagined the sheer longevity of the stuff? Everything drowned, and what lives on? Towering plastic stalagmites, strewn with rotting human gargoyles. Plastic. It rises up out of the depths of the waters to form grotesque new floating islands.

"Plastics Benjamin! 'Nuf said!"

The mouths of the rivers — the Petaluma, the Sonoma, the Napa — regurgitate into the San Pablo Bay. The long tongue of the American River is engorged, running crazy and unbound, across the wide lowlands of the Sacramento delta, flooding the landscape for miles in every direction. This swirling water is choked with garbage and human remains and mangled plastic objects. Every solid object and every rotting corpse from the crowded and technologically advanced era we had lived in, all of this refuse, things both biological and inanimate, was swept away by the forceful and repetitive Emperor Tides. Surging westwards, the big river and the smaller low-lying rivers, deposited their toxins — the last evidences of our last civilization — into the San Pablo Bay where they were swept farther into the San Francisco Bay. Former.

How do I know this?

I know.

I watched it all float past my treehouse. Hours of fun. Better than TV.

You could go crazy.

First the rivers suck the waters inland then, sated, they over-flow back into the bay and flow out to sea, not peacefully, not rhythmically in their natural tidal courses, but horrifically. The rivers collected their dead burdens. The rivers spoke to me with their newly powerful hydraulic energy.

You could go crazy.

Dogs, cats, puppies, kittens, cattle, horses.

God, the beauty of the horses. Even as their carcasses floated back and forth in the tides, and with each sunrise/sunset, moonrise/moonset, back and forth, inland and out to sea again, it was the horses that lasted longest in the tides until nothing but fetlocks jutted up here and there and sometimes caught the sun-light on those broken, torn, white bones — those fetlocks were all that remained of gorgeous racing limbs. They are prey ani-mals. Did you know that? Such huge fleet creatures, prey to the predators.

The horses: you could go crazy.

A house floated by. The whole damn thing. Front porch. Dormer windows intact. Kitchen sink visible, faucet and all. Stately and very slowly. A whole house.

You could go crazy.

Huge California Live Oak trees, majestic with one hundred years of top-growth, were uprooted and floated, in procession, like bishops in their vestments, floated with their leafy canopies reaching for the sky or maybe reaching for fresh air. These once-living trees formed a majestic, sacrificial parade in honor of the relentless tides. And, of course the dead — dead rats and skunks and raccoons alongside the dead minions of people — whole families, whole neighborhoods, former grocery shoppers, former customers of big box stores, all of them, all, swallowed up in The Emperor Tides. One thing was as vulnerable as the next. It did not matter to these tides. All of it flowed, unmoored, sometimes unrecognizable, into the San Pablo Bay. All dead. All drowned. All wrecked.

You could go crazy.

But you know what? I did not go crazy.

Well, maybe just a little. But who was there, in fact, to diagnose my behavior, or to put me on the spectrum, or to be offended if I screamed or cried or simply sat staring for blank hours, watching the water and its diminishing yet still fetid tidbits as they floated past my treehouse?

Who was left to say I was crazy?

Or not?

If survival is any sign of sanity, then I could say I had not gone crazy. But if survival was simply a sign of the tenacity of my particular metabolism, or of some strand in my DNA, or even of my propitious choice of this treehouse for my safety, then even I could not tell if I had or I had not gone crazy. I knew only one thing: that I survived.

You could go crazy.

Or you could starve.

What I discover is this: crazy is possible. But hunger is urgent.

All these things — the dead, the rotting, the horrors, the simple loneliness — it's all just ballast for the real job of keeping the body afloat, i.e., alive. Soon enough, hunger takes the place even of sheer desperate madness. And soon enough, you are engaged with the world again, foraging for food and water, just like your ancestors. Desperate. Hungry. The urgency of life is stoked by hunger long before it is nourished by art, and very long indeed, before it succumbs to crazy.

I know these things.

I'm here, aren't I?

Thanks to Jerry Sterns, I had a modest cache of canned beans. But I soon enough discovered that it would not last long if I continued eating at accustomed levels. So, I was sparing with my rations. Water, now that was no problem at all. Except that I had to be scrupulous about using the purification and desalinization tablets when I drew water from the incoming, only the incoming, tides. Outgoing tides were filthy. Plus, Epps, in his compulsive perfectionism, had set me up with a backup water collection system.

Really quite clever it was, although resembling a Rube Goldberg contraption, it was made with one of my smaller paintings. Epps stripped the canvas off the stretcher bars, rolled it into a funnel, and mounted it above the roof. The point of this funnel dipped into a collecting bottle. The top of the funnel was attached to three of the upper limbs of the oak by guy wires, and although the canvas blew around in the wind, it held fast and worked like a sail catching the bay breezes and moving about gracefully overhead. Epps had also attached a little garden chime to one of the wires so that I would take note if it were not tinkling, which would mean that the setup had broken and needed my attention for repairs. What was funneled into the bottle was good old-fashioned San Francisco fog, pure and clean and plentiful still. To access this water I had to climb up the ladder to the top of my treehouse where Epps had built a catwalk to get over to the funnel and bottle, so I could switch out the filled water bottle with an empty. Voila! Fresh water!

Vain and glorious man! He had anticipated everything.

Ah, art. How wonderfully my paintings have worked for me. No mere monument to ego or creativity, my oeuvre, so to speak, was actually and truly a 'work' which kept me alive for several, as it turned out, years. Much better than gallery representation with all the politics and bad wine. My paintings were clearly on view, had there been anybody to see them, foolish and beautiful remains of another time, another era. And now those paintings had the added cachet of being, actually useful for something. How many artists can say that? Not even the mysterious and smiling Mona Lisa was 'useful' in any way, shape, or form. So, take that Leonardo!

Well, after so many months of eating just a dab of beans here and a spoonful there, I reckoned that I would need another source, or other sources, for food. And what does the flood provide? All the fish in the sea.

Great schools of some variety of small fish swam past my treehouse as the tides flowed in and as the tides flowed out. I laid myself down on my stomach on my deck and watched their comings and goings, and here is what I discovered. First, I had nothing better to do than to watch fish swim by. But more important: these schools of fish, small silvery fish about the size of anchovies, had a kind of group consciousness, and with their bulging eyes, they seemed to be seeking my attention. They would swim in massive s-formations, undulating closer to my tree trunk, then hovering in the waters, they would look up at me. Or so I believed. But I soon enough began to delude myself that they were trying to communicate with me and that they were sympathetic to my hunger pangs, or maybe they actually could, indeed, hear the rumblings of my stomach through the sonar of their group intelligence. Intelligence?

Well, or so it seemed to me.

And what, pray tell, were they communicating across our species divide?

"Eat me."

Just like in Alice in Wonderland.

"Eat me."

Oh, I really was quite mad, as in crazy.

But what the hey!

Experimentally, I discovered that when the tide was high, I could dip a bucket into one of these schools of all the fish in the sea, and voila, it was so easy. These fish were such slow swimmers and so, well, willing for me to capture them — as it seemed in my emergent dementia — and, though it took a leap of faith on my part, I tossed a couple of purification tabs into their water, to clean them somewhat. I hoped. Then I reached into the bucket of still living creatures, I grasped one of them by thumb and forefinger — it was still alive and wiggling — and I slugged it down my throat. Maybe it died instantly from contact with my raging gastric juices, but I did not feel it wriggle down my gullet. It simply slid down, easy as anchovies from a pizza and not nearly as salty.

I waited.

For my inaugural taste of these fish, I was careful to eat only one and then I waited. If I die, I die.

But I did not die.

After twelve hours, just to be on the safe side, I decided to dine again. Now the fish were less lively in their bucket of water. So, I named them, just like Adam in the garden, I named them Slow Fish. At long last, and taking into consideration my being secular and all, I could see the logic of naming things. Helps keep one thing apart from another, yes?

Then there was the kudzu. My soup, my tea, my Praetorian Guard.

As the months went by, I watched a new species of vine grow up around outcroppings in the water. Wherever there was a plastic monument sticking up out of the water, and assuming it had a teaspoon of soil and a few clumps of dead human or animal remains stuck to it, up popped this new plant, looking for all the world like kudzu. This plant was new to the San Pablo Bay. These wetlands had never been known to host kudzu. With my handy-dandy set of dictionaries — remember me toting up hundreds of books to use as insulation for the treehouse? Good thing I did. I have ended up with quite a credible library. I looked up kudzu and discovered that it's a fast-growing Asian vine, Pueraria lobata, of the legume family, that is used for forage and erosion control and is often a serious weed problem in the southeastern United States.

Well.

That started a train of thought.

It's a legume. Bean stalk. As in 'Jack and The.' So, kudzu might have some value as a leafy green, or even as another source of protein for me. Flipping through my plant book, I discover that kudzu has all sorts of varieties and contains all sorts of 'natural' remedies. Bingo! Of course, it also dawned on me, that whichever one that this new species was, it was obviously thriving on human garbage and waste and who knows what brands of old or new toxins. There would be no way to determine the kudzu's nutritional value without my becoming my own guinea pig. So great, right? What's it going to do? Kill me? I should be so lucky.

Kidding. Just kidding.

The kudzu — I could see with my binoculars at this moment — was about a mile away, thriving and climbing up one of those weird structures formed by plastic objects and God knows what all. And so I began a long and slow waiting game. I would have to wait and see if the kudzu would somehow migrate over to my tuft of mud and tree trunk before I could start the experiment. It might be a long wait while the plant slowly migrated over here to my treehouse. Oh well. Long and slow I could manage. What choice did I have?

And so, my days unfolded. By now Epps had been gone for many weeks, perhaps months. I don't know. I lost count.

Anyways.

I had gone through the repertoire of grieving set out by Elisabeth Kübler-Ross in her cheering bedside tome, "*On Death and Dying.*" Boy. Wouldn't you have loved to have sat down next to her at your favorite watering hole? Bundle of laughs. Life of the party. Ha! See! See what happens when it's a devastating flood, and you're the last man standing? Watering hole? Who'd have known? Punning's the last remnant of your humanity to go down.

As I said, anyways.

Slow and steady wins the race. I organized my days around: survival, staying sane, sheer terror, utter despair, keeping well, sitting, sleeping, weeping, screaming — and now a new task to add to my schedule — watching with my binoculars the very slow progress, in my direction, of the distant kudzu vines.

They did not disappoint.

Whether it was by seed or by a tiny cutting that drifted across the mile of deep water, a leaf or two appeared at the base of my tree, under water by several feet, but visible during low tide to the naked eye. Ah ha! We were in business.

But, as in all things that you wish for, be careful thereof. In less than twenty-four hours, this slip of a plant had grown several feet in height and the same in breadth. Its tendrils moved with animal grace, grasping and hoisting itself ever upward, so that after several more hours, the sucker was half way up my stairs and grasping the handrails, without, I would like to point out, without the support of finials. Epps would have been pleased. Built to last.

I could see that unless I took the upper hand with this vine, it would eventually eat me instead of the other way around. But it also began to dawn, that maybe I could harness the power of this plant to engage it as a kind of Praetorian Guard for my tree-house. I figured it was simply a matter of time before an assortment of invasive intruders would come my way and I might need to fend them off somehow. Sure, I had firearms, courtesy of Jerry Sterns. And God knows he had done his best to make me into a marksman — person, person — marks-person, but I was uncertain about whether or not I could use my tools and my skills to actually shoot someone. I felt that I needed something else to back me up. I knew that I had better prepare for an onslaught of aggressive villains, creeps, zombies, sociopaths, nutcases, survivalists, conspiracy theorists, prison escapees, and disaster tourists. If I were to survive, I would need something unexpected, something unique, in my arsenal. Hence, Kudzu. Not only to eat, but to enlist as the guardian of my treehouse.

My plan was to advance on kudzu on two fronts: as food and as colleague or protector. Maybe I could enlist the kudzu as my own Praetorian Guard.

First the food part.

It would be conducted in two stages, I figured. First, raw. Then cooked. I thought kudzu might be more palatable and more nourishing cooked, like collard greens or spinach. But raw would come first. Let's get on with it: I picked a leaf and popped it right down my throat, raw.

Argh!

It was thoroughly vomit-making, wriggling and struggling, worlds more determined not to be eaten than Slow Fish. I urped it up, spitting and drooling.

Well. Into the stewpot with you, my friend.

In all my rambling, I may have neglected telling you about my cooking arrangements. They are sparse, and since I feared setting the whole place on fire, I rarely attempted using the camp stove that Sterns had given to me.

For the cooking method, here's what I did:

First, I thoroughly watered down a section of my deck, outside and as far from tree branches as I could manage; this was, after all a treehouse. I sloshed several buckets of water all around the spot where I intended to set alight the stove — it came with a single collapsible pot and its own matching collapsible lid. I added water and water purification and desalinization tabs. The brew came to a slow boil.

I grabbed and yanked at the kudzu and got a whole stem of it, which seemed to enrage the rest of the plant. It fought back mightily. Yet I got the upper hand. I felt that I had established some sort of hierarchy of power with the thing and it shrank back as if to say:

"Sir, Yes Sir!"

Then I tossed the stem into my little boiling pot and, whack, on with the lid for a good long boil.

As I had hoped, the kudzu gradually settled down in the boiling water. As it heated up, it gave up the fight, resigned to be cooked like spinach, I suppose. Cautiously peering into the pot, I spooned up a leaf or two for the tasting.

It tasted much like spinach and provided a decent broth to which I added salt tabs for flavoring. Soup du jour!

Hunger drives creativity. Yes? It also dispels any 'ick-factor' about what is food and what is simply Nature's ornamentation. Imagine how hungry the first person to eat a lobster must have been.

When I go up onto the catwalk to check on my water bottle and funnel, I can see my world from about twenty feet higher than from my deck. This rooftop aerie allows me to see the view to the west and much farther to the south than from my east-facing front deck. I take my binoculars with me. They swing back and forth on a stout, braided, water-proof lanyard that Jerry Sterns had included with my survival gear. The water-proof part was, I like to believe, a little joke from him to me. Got it, Jerry. Very funny.

With the binoculars' high-powered lenses, I can see the outlines of two of the Bay Area's highest mountains: Mount Diablo and Mount Tamalpais. But my glasses are not quite powerful enough to detect any possible human activities on either of these outcroppings. What is so exasperating for me, the lone survivor so-called, is that I cannot discern if there are other survivors who might have gone uphill to one or the other of these peaks. At this point the mountains are islands, completely surrounded by water. During the high and low tides, they appear to rise or sink as the water alternately engulfs them higher uphill or lower downhill. All I can see is their dusky golden silhouettes, familiar landmarks, now hovering, peculiar and strange, in an archipelago.

Mount Tamalpais used to be at an altitude of 2572 feet above the old sea level. And Mount Diablo was at 3848 feet above former sea levels. These mountain landmarks are the highest points that I can view from my treehouse. I never heard a definitive report on how high the seas rose around those peaks before all communication systems ceased. And you know what? Frankly, I don't care. Right now, to me, lone survivor or not, those mountain landmarks are simply distant islands. I don't know and, really, cannot afford to care, if anybody else is out there. I've got my routine to maintain: got work cut out for me to keep myself and this treehouse enterprise going.

There are times when The Emperor Tides come up perilously close to the floor of my treehouse and other times when I can splash around in the muddy swamplands below it, in my waders.

Anyways.

One fine morning, I am up on the catwalk, squinting into my binoculars in the direction of Mount Tam, when an enormous hen swoops down — she is actually flying quite gracefully — and she lands on the catwalk, fluffs up her feathers and commences to lay an egg. I know all the signs. I used to keep hens. The fact that she swooped down, gracefully or not, was quite a miracle as hens have had their wing muscles bred out of them to facilitate generations of farmer's wives who had hoped to keep the hens in or near the hen house to facilitate egg-collecting. The tale of the domestic hen is not a happy one. This hen had unusually strong wings and she used them. As soon as she is done laying her egg on my rooftop, she flaps mightily and off she goes, up, up and away. And there it is: an egg.

Well, at this point, it had been a month of Sundays since I had eaten an egg, maybe longer. I approached it, stealthily, as if sneaking up on some prey or other. And there it was, warm and wobbling on the boardwalk, formerly called my catwalk, but suddenly destined to be re-christened The Hen Roost. An egg, an egg! Today was the high point of my life in my treehouse thus far.

An egg.

How to cook it?

I was not sure I could even remember how to make an egg: scrambled, boiled, sunny side up, over easy? So many options for my single egg.

I began to tremble in a kind of violent shaking seizure. My body was so hungry for protein, I suppose, and my mind in such a state of deprivation, that I grabbed the lovely thing, bit down on the small end, and swallowed that lone egg, whole, in a single gulp. I even experimented with a few morsels of egg shell. Repellant as it may sound, those calcium-loaded shards actually felt good crunching among my molars.

I ate it raw. I ate the whole thing. The high point of my day.

Then there is this: solitude

Now I step into the deep waters of trouble. I simply cannot resist the urge to pun in describing what came next. The flood is so rich in cornball associations. We were truly out to sea with what came next.

After the King Tides of California, so many years ago, then came the deluge! Thank you dear Louis Quinzième!

Now that I was completely immersed in The Emperor Tides, I was blindsided by what was to come next.

Solitude.

But nobody could have anticipated, nor come up with an ad slogan for the solitude that came of being left up shit creek without the proverbial. As for solitude, it turned out to be, for me, a whole 'nuther' thing.

One minute you're building a charming little garden folly, all la-dee-da with optimism and hope, and enjoying a bit of a frisson over your builder. The next minute you are foolish enough to think you might actually be building a structure which will actually save your life.

Fools, all of us.

Me especially.

So let's get serious, now.

No joke, this.

It's not whether you can find enough to eat. Find enough to drink. Keep from going mad.

It is whether, or not, you can abide solitude. Not just privacy. Not just a few moments to think in peace. But whether, and if, you can abide being in a world without any person-made sounds. Whether, and if, you can just sit there and be bored senseless at times. That, in between bouts of sheer terror, desperate thirst, wobbling hallucinations, drowsy ennui, and crazy hopefulness — that is your life if you are a lone survivor.

It's not all fishing for food and collecting water. Most of it is just sitting on your butt and being alone. Sure. You think you'd love a few quiet moments. But so many moments? How many can you take? No distant airplane drones. No automobiles honk. Not the sound of tires on gravel. Hi, Honey, I'm home. No phones, for God-sakes — not one! No overhearing the neighbors, whining at one another, 'honey can you do me a HUGE favor.' No dogs barking. No doors slamming. Not a distant TV with daytime confections for the bored influenza sufferer. Not the cat quietly crunching dry cat food in the kitchen. Not even the anticipation of sounds.

Oh, there are rustling leaves and cracking tree limbs. Birds. Nice. Very nice. But how much can a girl take of silence? A silence which has become the sole stand-in for human activity.

Solitude?

I am not even so sure I would name this new state of being with such a nice word as 'solitude'. With its hint of poems being thought up or paintings finding their way onto canvas. Solitude? A nice therapeutic moment alone? No, solitude is too nicey-nice for what this kind of being alone consists of.

And yet, solitude — for lack of a better word — is the one and the most unexpected result of catastrophe. All the Hollywood movies in the world did not mention the solitude to you: the survivor of the atomic bomb, of Frankenstein, of Godzilla, of the plague, of the raging inferno, of the flood.

Ha! The flood! Who would have had the creative imagination back then — what screenwriter of that era — could have flashed on how solitude would really feel, how it could destroy mere contentment, could precipitate madness?

Little old silent solitude.

Believe me it was no picnic.

Are you bothered by my trite simile? Do I care? Do I care if this future reader is annoyed by my clichés? You, cliché-less critic of my clichés. Do you know what I think of you? You are the cliché. With your judgements about my life after The Emperor Flood. Feh!

That's why I started writing about all this.

Because there was nothing else to do.

Long hours of nothing to do.

At first, I slept a lot. I could fall asleep any time. Not a nice salubrious little nap. Ah, how lovely. I feel all better now. Not like that. My sleeps were a muzzy dark form of despair. I do believe that's not too dramatic a word: despair. Not given to the trials of drama queens, I am punctilious about the words they used back then, before The Emperor Flood. I could never stand the kind of gal who, first of all refers to herself as a 'gal', but who, with hand to fevered brow, whines about how depressed she is. How you, her bestest friend, could never IMAGINE what she's been through. Thus, I am suspicious of myself when I use the word 'despair' to describe my naps, my sleeps, especially early on in my solitude.

Solitude.

Such a nice soft little word.

Hell.

I was not just a sole survivor. Experiencing my solitude. I was a sick demented raging lab rat maniacally and uselessly tapping the lever hoping to get a reward, any reward — anything to help me escape this dreaded solitude.

Worn out, I slept. I slept the sleep of the prisoner sentenced to 'solitude'.

Then, one afternoon, waking up in my own drool, I simply got up, unsnapped the cover on my Underwood typing machine — gift of one of Berkeley's longest-lived Ph.D. candidates, Eugene Hampton — and I started to type.

At first, I wouldn't call this new activity 'writing'. It was mostly just banging on the keys. First to flex my fingers. Then to get the right pressure of my fingers on the keyboard, to get a rhythm going. This old keyboard needed muscle to function. Not like your buttery old computer keyboard. Thank the gods for junior high school typing class. Yes?

A-s-d-f-g-h-j-k-l-;

The most useful skill I ever learned, typing. God knows quadratic equations bit the dust. And memorizing the dates of Civil War battles, gone with the wind, if you don't mind another feeble joke. But typing. Now there's a skill you never lose. Worlds more useful than riding a bike.

That's why I started writing about all this.

Because there was nothing else to do.

Long hours of nothing to do. An overdose of solitude.

Typing: a most useful skillset.

Skillset! Don't you love it? Twenty-first century word inventions: lifestyle, sleep systems, flavor profiles, selfies, 'issues'. We were so over-euphemized by the time the floods came round that nobody knew what to call them. 'Issues' with mother nature? 'Concerns" about the tides? Adaptations to weather-o-logical conditions?

Here's a thought: maybe that's why I don't mind trite similes and clichés. At least they are simple, clean and understandable. Not a pseudo-intellectual mishmash or technobabble. Not politically correct mannerisms affected so as to not hurt anybody's delicate sensibilities.

I am alone. Not many people around here to worry about my insulting them with mere words.

Let's give this writing a try:

I live on despite the circumstances. Despite the flood. Or maybe I live on because of the flood. What do you think about that notion?

Maybe the outrageous impossibility of my continued lifespan is because I have had something to fight against, to rage against, to get my blood flowing and heart beating, an event so unimaginable that my mind itself has been engaged in thinking, thinking, thinking and that all this extreme activity of staying alive, with my own rapid terrified heartbeats, with my own pumping blood pressure, with my own pulsing brain cells;

maybe all this forced activity has actually preserved my organism and that's why I am surviving?

Or not.

You see where solitude takes you.

It's enough to make you believe in God.

Or not.

Mostly not, I think.

But it is definitely enough to make you mad at God. That's me, alright. Madder than hell.

And so?

So I started typing.

Here's how it went:

At first my typing was to exercise my fingers. Later to create meaning; to describe. I started typing about my situation, stuck here above endless surging water in my own sturdy treehouse. Keeping track of how I survived and how I felt and so forth and so on.

Then, once my fingers were limber enough to resume touch typing as a manifestation of internalized thinking, I started to type about my feelings. About how upset I was. How angry I was. How lonesome I was. Things like that for starters. Typing on my typewriter became a form of physiotherapy where, out from my fingertips spewed the contents of my brain and mind and my entire being, if such things were possible. And it was a clean pursuit, cleansed as it were, by the impossibility of it, my typing, ever becoming literature. So I was cleared of the pretensions of creativity or of any form of artistic aspiration. I was typing, with no grand objectives in view, but, still, seeing all the things that I have seen from my treehouse, I was making a record of them. It's beyond vocabulary. It has been so horrible, and, well, 'horrible' is such a small word isn't it? Had I the requisite pretentions to writing well of this event, of my life, post The Emperor Floods, well then, at least I might have taken out my battered Thesaurus; found another juicier word than threadbare 'horrible'.

A baby floated by. I tell you! It was still in its hospital incubator attached to tubes and monitors, cables and wires snaked behind the machine, whipping and lunging in and out, in and out, of the surging black water. An infant. Blue and rigid. A baby, I tell you!

You could go crazy.

Did I go crazy?

Have I gone crazy?

And I flash on the old, old story.

I remember that another baby was said to have floated by. A baby in a basket.

Class?

Moses, of course.

Drawn out of the water, alive, he was alive. Not like the baby I saw down there in the black swirling waters of The Emperor Tides.

That long-ago baby in the basket, was destined to be the hero of our stories. And I start wondering who saved him?

So, I'm obliged to review that old story, seeing a baby floating by my own dwelling; a nightmare baby, dead, but still evocative of a story dimly remembered; the pivotal story of our Jewish psyches, secular or not.

Here's my take on that old, old story:

Midrash Two: Baby in a Basket

Pharaoh's daughter, and a princess of his court, sees a baby float by, a baby in a basket and she saves the baby Moses then persuades her father to let the baby be nursed by Moses' own mother, Jahokved. But why? Why would she, daughter of a tyrannical Pharaoh, even care about saving a passing infant, a boy-baby, subject to her own father's cruel edict? Why did she save that baby? Let me suggest, if I may, how this might have gone for her.

By the way, I remember that her name was Bitya. How come I remembered that? She says to me:

"You ask me why? Here are some things to consider: I am the daughter of the tyrant Pharaoh, but I am also the daughter of a mother. My mother's name is not mentioned in your stories. Neither is her tribe named. If I say she was an Israelite who had worked in the palace of my father, cleaning the night soil, could you picture that he may have had his way with her? Could you say that I am, then, the daughter of an Israelite? And since Israelite heritage is determined by the mother, could you then believe that I had my mother's blood flowing in my heart? If this were true, I could say that I truly had a vested interest in saving the baby boy that I found floating by in the water. The Israelite women were trying to preserve the lives of their newborn infants, some of those mothers sent them downstream, in baskets, for fate to find them somewhere safe to survive, far away from Pharaoh's, my father's, evil pronouncements. I knew that this baby in a basket was an Israelite. I too was an Israelite woman. I saved his life!"

A baby floated by.

You could go crazy.

In my real-life version of floating babies, it was a dead baby. No wonderment was possible in my version. No heroes. No literature.

A baby floated by my treehouse. It was dead.

Naturally, I flash on Moses. Or should I say, unexpectedly I flash on Moses. These old stories are hard to shake, even under the direst of circumstances. I could go crazy. Maybe so.

So what's with this Pharaoh and his edicts anyway? Kill the boy-children. Let the girl-children live? What's with these pharaonic fathers?

Oh, I realize, I do, that not every father embodies Pharaoh's brand of treachery.

Taking Moses in the basket and Pharaoh's daughter, look how that turned out. Even if she was not the daughter of an Israelite as I imagine. Yet she defied her father. Took the infant, thus committing an individual act of civil disobedience against her father's edicts. And Moses thrived.

So too, I would like to believe, did Pharaoh's daughter which says to me 'yes' even a murderous father can produce strong and independent female offspring.

Poster child for that kind of parent: me.

Do I have too much time to think? Quit griping, I say. Thinking was what I had originally wanted with my treehouse.

Truth and Beauty

So what's with them? Aren't truth, capital T. and beauty, capital B, overwhelmed by disaster? Surely Disaster wipes out Truth and Beauty.

Oddly, no.

It goes like this.

In the Hollywood version of Disaster, they don't tell you about how the lone survivor ends up with all the time in what's left of an uncertain world to think. More important, the survivor has all the time at the end of the world to just sit and stare. At what?

The beauty of my mornings.

I weep.

I do.

The beauty of the rising sun as it illuminates, in their dancing millions, the tiny jewels that ride the chop of the endless waters. My mornings reveal that the earth is still spinning, moving in its habitual way to reveal the sun that resides 93 million miles from my treehouse. What a paucity of vocabulary I have for describing this aching beauty. Maybe my mornings are more beautiful than they used to be, prior to The Emperor Flood, because of that baby floating by, in its once life-sustaining coffin. Maybe my mornings are more beautiful because I am alone. The beauty of the sun making the water to sparkle. The demonstrable fact of the cosmos that the earth moves even this day. I am moved by its steadfastness, the earth that spins. Even now, turns on its axis. And me the only human person to see this event. Earth turns to reveal sunrise. And it's my habit to watch it. But, given all the time in the world to think about it, it's not the sun that rises, but the turning of the earth that makes it seem like the sun is rising. The sun is still that monster star that is simply out there moving ever-outward on its expanding course after the Big Bang. The sun is not rising. It is being revealed. Its aching beauty. Sad beauty. Habitual. Repetitive, the revelation of the sun yet again, on this new day, being 'revealed' over its ruined water-scape. And only one human being to articulate, or to try to articulate, its beauty on this particular morning, again.

'Morning. Morning. Feel so lonesome in the morning.'

Sadly sang Richie Havens in commemoration of mornings, so long ago.

And Truth?

What about that conundrum?

The truth of the human being, in social groupings or all sole, alone; the truth of the human being is excretion. Urine and shit. Jerry Stearns, a bit prissy when it came to speak of these things, he preferred to call them 'outgoing'. He had provided me with several buckets, various sizes. And the two largest of them were for, Jerry's words: Incoming and Outgoing.

Incoming buckets were for gathering water during the incoming tides. Incoming tides were somewhat less laden with human detritus than outgoing tides. The incoming waters required detox and desalinization tabs to create passable drinking water.

The Outgoing bucket, a big one, was for human waste, for me to deposit with the outgoing tides.

And so my beautiful mornings were interrupted with chores. The chores of dealing with the truth of human beings. Shit and urine. Tossing it out. Sloshing the bucket out. Careful not to lose it in the tidal surges. And returning it for another day's use.

And then the sunsets. Reverse of sunrise. But now a new beauty is revealed.

The best thing about being sole survivor after a catastrophe, that destroys whole cities, is the night sky. Without the distracting ambient glow of city skyscapes, I could see stars in their billions. And I would sit there looking east. Sometimes I fell asleep lying on my side facing east and woke later to see that the whole canopy of stars had moved a few ticks to the south since my last being awake. My mind's eye would do a little fast forward and, zip, the stars moved. Except, of course, it was not the stars who had moved, but the earth that had spun.

'Evening. Evening. Feel so lonesome in the evening.'

Richie Havens sang to me.

Today I feel vibrantly healthy. There is a vibrating rainbow shimmer around the edges of the leaves in my tree. The sky is unbearably cerulean. It has been many weeks, or is it months, since I have felt so able to move my arms and legs with my muscles so taut and well oiled. My knees feel as if they could spin in a full circle. I feel so good. Finally, I can think and by this, I mean my brain is clicking and racing; a buzzing little motor with a spinning flywheel. Today I shall clean house. Organize my stuff. Maybe do a little creative cooking. Catch Slow Fish.

Write in this book. Do research on the rivers of California. Research weather for the past twenty-five years

An odd thing just happened.

Is happ

In my center field of vision, I am blind.

Took many time to type that

If I move my head I can see this page of typing, but only with big blotches of blank paper floating from side to side. Hard to type.

Weird

took acetaminophen. Lie don

Am shiver

Hot sweat

Sick teet h chat ter ing

sick

Day 2 bad

D3 bad sic

s

s

s

Bad

sick, bad

Sick bad

ok bad

ok bett

better

So what was that about?

Today is first day I can thnk

Still part blind with patches of blank as I read this.

How many days? Last memory ten days then faint or what?

More days have past. Undramatic pain in belly. Much part blindness. Big dots on paper. Ears ring. Mouth numb. Drooling. Teeth ache. Chills. Fever. Aspirin and alka seltzer. No new

Danny is here

I think – think Daniel made me sick. Sick think. Sicking made me thick. I see him. He here

Dan

D

Help me

Think dan made me sick

Danny

Dan

d

I am back.

I do not know how long I was sick. I do not know what kind of illness it was. I may have forgotten to put decon tabs in water. Or maybe fishes had sickness inside them. Much hallucination. Much shiver and fever. Chattering and painful teeth. Much partial blindness with blobs floating around my field of vision.

Fool that I am, I tried repeatedly to write about things in the moment and I see that little was recorded. What? Am I writing for posterity? Me the last man standing? Woman. Sorry. Woman. But you get what I mean. I am considerably foggy still. I don't even care what this sounds like. Feh!

Then somehow, I, in effect, woke up from my illness. It was quite worse than flu. Worse than food poisoning. Not quite a stomach thing. Not quite a heart attack. Very migraine-ish. But worse. Pain in teeth and jaw. Drooling. Breathing, thick and gasping. Nightmares. Hallucinations? Could not eat. Had to force myself to stay hydrated by choking and retching up water. Licked salt from emergency meds. Salt was disgustingly retchingly sick-making in my tongue and throat, but I thought I needed salt. Somehow managed to put purification tabs in water before drinking. Pains in bones – hip crests, humorous, jaw, and small bones in feet – grinding dull pain. Sweating profuse on neck and chest, drenching. I would have happily died.

I lived.

In the middle of the night upon the onset of wellness, I sat up. I had been sleeping or had passed out, on the floor with no blanket, no pillow. I was filthy and my flesh smelled bad. But when I woke up from this sickness, it was over. Gone. I felt well-being. I felt well. It was over.

I stood up, wobbly, and fell back onto the floor. But I felt good. I needed to be clean. I managed to wobble across the room to the out bucket and across the room to the in bucket. Both were almost empty. Shaking violently, but feeling well and happy, I felt happy, I cannot believe it. I felt happy. I managed to carry the buckets to the deck and fling them both overboard, holding their chains; I was strong, revived. I rinsed them out in what I discerned was an incoming, cleaner, tide. And here's another weird thing.

The kudzu had not grown at its usual pace during whatever time it was that I had been sick. It seemed to be waking up too and to be re-assessing its own health. As if it, too, had been sick and had languished on its way up the stairs. Its leaves were grey and limp. Its tendrils somewhat dried out on the tips. And as I woke up more thoroughly, it too seemed to be waking up. We greeted each other, in a fashion, with a nod here and there and it was as if my faithful kudzu were saying:

"Hey, you look much better, Sarah Steinway. Glad to see you're back."

"Hello, kudzu, you too, you faithful Praetorian Guard."

The vine drew upward as if to attention. Its leaves brightened. Its tendrils waved as if to greet me. As if this were really, truly happening. I was, indeed, quite lost, quite mad.

Then the sun began to rise and I looked down at the tide and my buckets were cleansed and I dragged them back up by their chains and threw the incoming bucket of water over my head and I sat there on the floor of my deck and watched the sun rise and the new waters flow in.

Had I gone truly quite mad? Me and my kudzu? This was crazy thinking. But I felt well again.

Elvis Sightings.

How do you know when you're hallucinating? No. Really. How?

I'm asking.

Have you ever had an hallucination? Well then, you, child of the sixties, you know full and well why I'm asking.

That hand that had turned into a skeleton as it reached for your head and you jerked back, terrified. It was so real you had said, shuddering. That's why I'm asking.

You might observe that, since I'm asking, I am okay. Right?

So okay, then. You're okay, then?

You mean that I'm pretty sane if I know enough to ask.

But wait.

If I tell you I really, really, really saw Elvis you'd start backing away.

"Yeah, but he was so real! I saw him. Swear to God. Sparkle suit and all!"

No, not the sparkle suit.

It was him, young again, a regular trailer trash middle-brow ducktail-handsome greaser. And he was right here. Standing where you're standing. And he was moaning some song about how he loves me. I mean he LOVES ME and I can see it in his eyes. It's me he's singing to. Just me.

Only thing is: here I am alone in my treehouse. And it's about a million years since Elvis died. And I'm about a million years older. And that skinny teenage punk is deader than dead. In fact, that beautiful punk who was standing right here in front of me, who was crooning love lyrics to me, just me, that boy was dead to Elvis long before Elvis was dead to the world.

But he was so real. Realer than real.

It is with the aforementioned proviso, that I tell you about my visitors: if they are hallucinations, I am quite mad. If they are real, I am in for real trouble. Either way, it's a slippery slope.

Intruder.

It wasn't like in the movies. I assure you.

I gotta say, for all the world's big three religions, with the ten words on the tablets and all that; for all the honoring of those ten commandments, there sure was a lot of killing in our world back then before The Emperor Tides. Or murder, if you prefer that word to 'killing'. Murder, the word, with its connotation of preconceived planning and thinking about murder before actually murdering a person. Or persons. But I quibble.

Not only was the pre-Emperor Tides world drenched in murderous bloodshed, it was every day. Every day a new killing and/or a new mass murder scene in the news. And not just single souls, or the armies, sent off to meet their bullets, but whole groups killed or murdered. Even school children blown to bits. I don't care what you call it, dead bodies were the result. You saw murdered people all the time before The Emperor Tides. Did I become numb to all the carnage? I suppose so on some subconscious level.

Thus, dear reader, when it came to the murder that I myself committed, I would have thought that I had been well prepared to be quite indifferent to the act. Killing and murder were rampant in the last throes of our civilization, so-called.

The surprise was this, then: when I was confronted with dangerous, irrational, starving, crazy human beings who were obviously bent on killing me and taking my treehouse, my home, I swung into action like a professional soldier, using all the skills that Jerry Sterns had taught me.

"Okay so here's the thing Mrs. S. The thing of it is, is this…"

He paused for a moment as he placed a flat wooden box and a canvas shotgun bag on the ground at our feet. He turned a small key in the box-lock and snapped open the lid. The smell of gun oil rose suggestively from a balding velvet cloth that embraced a well-cared-for hand gun. Seeing the weapon, I looked away, far away at the water-flattened grassy ground where we stood. We were standing under what I used to call The Owl Tree. I'd rather look for owl pellets than learn how to shoot.

"So, the deal is this, Mrs. Steinway. You either shoot AT someone from your past or you shoot BECAUSE of someone from your past. That's my theory. Either way, that is your target, especially when you're first learning how to handle your weapon. Holding that thought, you will be more likely to hit what you are actually aiming at, now, in real time. It's focus I'm talking about here, Sarah. Ma'am. Nothing so focuses the mind and the eye of the shooter more effectively than something to focus upon. If you see what I mean. And I believe, and I've seen it a thousand times, the more the novice shooter uses his or her past life, her experiences, the more she employs those episodes to focus attention onto the target, while aiming well, while always holding the thought that you are shooting either AT someone from your past or shooting BECAUSE of someone from your past, well, the better shooter she will be. You see what I mean, don't you?"

I did not.

This was going to be a slog, if you don't mind another water-logged pun.

I was destined to be one of Jerry Sterns' worst marks-per-son-ship students. Whether I learned to shoot AT someone or BECAUSE of someone, it was soon more than evident that I did not have the requisite free associative skills. Past or no past. AT or BECAUSE were beside the point. I was hopeless.

I did, however, spy an owl pellet a few feet away from the trunk of the owl nesting tree. I scrabbled over to the specimen, scooped it up in my bare hands.

"What's that Mrs. Steinway?"

"Owls."

"What?"

"Jerry, it's an owl pellet. This used to be their nesting ground. Look. Look up there in the branches. That's where they used to perch."

Holding his hand gun at his side, barrel facing the ground, he craned his head up. We both looked up.

We stood there, companionable, trying to see up into the tree branches.

He scanned the tree branches skillfully. He was twelve years old, searching for owls.

"Maybe they've gone, Mrs. S."

"Probably, Jerry."

He lowered his gaze, sweeping down the gigantic tree trunks as he did so, and fastened me with an unblinking stare.

"You in love with Epps?"

What? The craziness! This was target practice. The nerve!

"I mean with the treehouse and all that, Mrs. S."

"Jerry. Please."

"I can ask, can't I?"

"No, Jerry. You can't."

I looked away. He bobbed his head to catch my eyes again.

"Look, Jerry. No, I'm not. Not a lot. Not at all."

And focusing on him, looking him in the eyes, I focused on my thoughts. And whether or not I was aiming my remarks A T him or BECAUSE of him, or AT or BECAUSE of anyone else in my life, I looked away, embarrassed.

"No. I am not. With Epps. In love."

"Yeah, Mrs. S. I thought so. Woman of valor, you are."

I can't help liking this guy. Paranoid, loud-mouth, crazy-making. He's everything and everyone I would never in a million years invite to my barbeque. Yet, I liked him. He was oddly comfortable somehow.

"Suit yourself, Mrs. S. Now. As to the subject at hand. As I said, you will either shoot AT somebody or BECAUSE of somebody. Either way, it sharpens the mind which, in turn, sharpens the gaze, which as a welcome corollary, sharpens your shot. You want to shoot sharp. That's where you get your word 'sharpshooter.' Did you know that Mrs. S?

He was a fount, was Jerry Sterns.

"Now let me just say this Mrs. S: this is not an arcade game. An intruder will intend to kill you. I am not kidding. It's not negotiable for you to allow an intruder into your shelter during or after the shit hits the fan. You won't need to ask why they are there. They are there to kill you. The very fact that they are there in your treehouse is all the proof you need to assure you that you must AIM WELL. In other words: always shoot to kill.

One thing, however.

That first intruder — I never fired a bullet.

As to my methods. Well, the first intruder, a straggly, filthy teenage girl to whom I initially thought I could perhaps offer safe harbor. But she threatened me with a shard of glass, whipping it in front of her body, back and forth, slashing the air, this way and that way, and ranting all the while, stepping closer with each wave of her shaking arm.

I was unprepared.

Like an idiot, I had not kept my pump action shotgun

loaded. But I edged across and to one side of the ragged movements of this girl, really, she was just a girl, and you got to feel humanity coming from her, yet she was too far gone from being nearly killed herself probably, any number of times out there, swimming, struggling in the rising waters and then, against all rational hope, she drags up my stairs, crazy and muddy, and she is armed with a shard of broken windowpane. I could not feel any humanity toward her except that she was eventually going to slash my flesh, and that is how survival kicked in to my formerly civilized little self.

I edged across the floor, kind of chanting, kind of talking softly the way I would to a rabid dog and finally got within grabbing distance of my shotgun. In one swift movement, I lifted it to my cheek and with a blind reflex racked the pump. It was loud. You may already know that sound. But it was loud enough to set the girl to trip, ungainly, backwards where her butt hit the deck handrail, and the velocity of her skinny body flipped her over the rail and backwards into the oncoming tide. I heard a loud cracking sound as she bounced backwards. Her neck or spine broke. I think. And she was gone.

I was shaking violently. I vomited. I wept. Long strands of my stomach contents dribbled down my shirt. I was still holding the shotgun, one hand welded to the pump mechanism, and after some moments, I do not know how many moments, I realized that I had vomited onto the shotgun too. Miserable. Misery. Worse. Worse than the worst thing I could ever remember happening to me. Worse than Daniel Robert Steinway slipping away and dying on our bed.

"You have your whole life ahead of you, Sarah", he had said

just before he died.

No.

I do not have my life, WHOLE, any more, Daniel.

Don't ask me about all this. Stop wondering.

I cracked that pump action three more times over the next year. That was the first year after The Emperor Tides propelled me onto the far side of humanity. After that, no more dangerous people came my way. And I could rest.

But some nights it was all I could do to not think about murder and my stomach would reflexively regurgitate my meager meals of Slow Fish and kudzu tea as I recalled the sounds of necks and backs cracking as they careened over the handrail of my deck.

I had in me hatred, repellant to think about, and it was physical. Since I had trained in the use of a shotgun with Jerry Sterns, I had prepared myself to kill and, therefore, it was premeditated murder that I did out here. It's true. Now, in addition to being a lone survivor, I was also a murderer. Not human any more in a San Francisco sort of woo-woo way, where we sat warming our hearts with Irish coffees, all cozy and whole and human and filled with noble liberal empathy and love-thy-neighbor sort of stuff.

NO.

After killing human beings, I was aware of what I had had inside me all along. It had probably hidden there, nascent, for my entire lifetime before The Emperor Tides stranded me in extreme danger and isolation. My talent for murder had been slumbering; perhaps nourishing itself for action, lying buried somewhere, inside my soul, until I was threatened. Then I discovered that my self, the person who I had believed myself to be, a person who was charming and thoughtful and discursive and sometimes mordantly humorous, that old self, my old self, was slashed and drained of blood as surely as I would have been if I had not murdered that first intruder, that girl waving a shaking piece of broken glass in my direction.

Now I was feral.

It happened on the morning of the girl-intruder. Ethics and gentle Buddha mindfulness, and all that non-violent nonsense crammed into books, it all vanished the moment someone tried to kill me. From that day forward I knew that I could shoot to kill, rather, that I would shoot to live.

-V-

Know where you came from:
know where you are going . . .
Do not forget anything your
eyes have seen.

Pirke Avot 3:1 & 3:8

BIRDS OF A FLOOD.

I had mentioned that my tree is intermittently home to flocks of birds, both wild and domestic, now gone feral. Generally, they gather in squabbling groups of-a-feather, they make eggs, hatch their young and protect their turf until the little ones fledge. Then they fly off to God-knows-where. Over the seasons that I've lived here, the bird populations have been winnowed by their own constant warfare for space and resources. Birds are not nice creatures. They have also been winnowed out by predators. Me for instance. I have become a dab hand with the slingshot Jerry Sterns had included in my SHTF kit. Every once in a while, I get an egg or two.

So birds.

Birds, as I just noted, are not nice creatures. Sure, back before The Emperor Floods, everybody had had bird feeders: for hummingbirds, doves, house finches, sparrows. As if birds couldn't, and hadn't, been able to forage for themselves over the millennia and gotten along just fine, thank you very much. What I had noticed, even back then when we were all home-grown ornithologists, and oh, aren't they just darling and oh, look at that one with yellow feathers! Even back then I could see that birds were in a constant state of warfare, squabbling, flapping at one another, stealing the eggs of their neighbors, eating, eating, eating! They would even dine on other birds' nestlings! Birds are not nice creatures I tell you. Flight warfare existed back then too. Ever watch hummingbirds battle at a feeding station? I rest my case. Birds of a feather may, indeed, nest together. But birds NOT of a feather cannot abide one another. Ever.

Then there were the domestic chickens that had gone feral. Who'd a thunk? So, there was the occasional chicken egg up there on my Hen Roost. Bliss!

But the worst episode of the birds of the The Emperor Tides was the battle Royale between the Egrets and the Sea Gulls. This occurred in the initial phases of the incoming and outgoing tides and we — my treehouse crew and I — watched it unfold with a mixture of wonder at the 'wonders' of Nature and pure disgust at the vicious spectacle.

We all know what disgusting scavengers Sea Gulls are. They fly in reeling formations over every dump in the world. They will dine on anything from restaurant garbage to old tee-shirts. They are filthy and they scream incessantly. They are agile and powerful fliers. And, the more pressed they are for resources — I discovered once I had moved into my treehouse — the more aggressive they become. As shore birds, they and the dainty Egrets, had abided one another for hundreds of years on the formerly broad edges of waterways and seasonal wetlands of the San Pablo and San Francisco Bays. But as shorelines were engulfed, feeding and breeding grounds shrank and then the Egrets became targets for the voracious Gulls. It was easy pickings for the gulls.

All they had to do — to increase both their nesting grounds and their source of fresh food — all they had to do was to swoop down and viciously bite at the long slender ankles of the wading Egrets. The bites of the gulls would not quite kill the Egrets. With swift runnels of blood rushing out of their leg wounds and with broken leg bones jutting at unbearable angles, the Egrets toppled over into the shallows. Some drowned immediately; a blessing. Others, with long necks lifting their lovely little heads out of the water, those were the worst off, and they screamed and thrashed. The poor injured Egrets would die slowly, but surely, victims of incoming masses of swarming gulls.

The gulls seemed to relish the live food source of the Egrets and they tugged and pulled at the living Egrets' intestines. The noise was so distressing to me, it made my stomach heave and I almost went crazy during the months of the Egret and Gull confrontations. Wars.

There were, of course, other species of birds fighting for territory and food early on in the gradually rising tides, but nothing got to me like the battle of the shore birds.

As if that were not enough, the gulls were soon joined by Pelicans. The Pelicans' skills as foragers of the shorelines and their greater wing spans and strength meant that the gulls had more than met their match. Pelicans won the high ground. Then almost immediately, lost it when the next series of The Emperor

Tides surged in and covered even these last bits of dry land. Plus, devils that they were, the Pelicans soon enough discovered the schools of Slow Fish and so I had my own territorial fight with them. A miserable time. Miserable.

You can see why I just might have a beef with God, now. How could He, She or It allow such cruelty? I ask you!

I'm mad I tell you!

In fact, I am mad enough to sit right down and argue with God, once and for all and right now. And, even though I do not have that cherished Jewish grudge against Hebrew school, which can morph into a grudge against God, and even though I can't fall back on that other Jewish grudge: the forty-year grudge against a nameless rabbi over a bar mitzvah — granted, not strictly an argument with God as such — but who can keep track of all these reasons to take issue with God? But, harbored and nurtured, these kinds of grudges get projected onto God. And the aggrieved victim — so-called, self-referentially — that person quits all things Jewish, including his God, over a bar mitzvah slight.

See what I mean?

And these grudges last a lifetime.

So here I am.

In an argumentative mood. About to argue with God.

It's the damn birds and their warfare, I tell you.

And I will argue with God!

Are you listening, God?

As if.

So. By now you know I'm not really mad; as in crazy. Maybe. Maybe not.

But you need to know I am genuinely mad; as in angry. And maybe you know why I am mad.

I told you. It's the birds. The damned birds and their bloody warfare.

And, who, pray tell, am I angry at? With nobody around, who's to be mad?

I am mad at God.

There.

Said it.

Done.

And you see, I am still here. No lightning strike to blow me away. Still here, I am. Still alive. Still here in my treehouse.

Midrash Three: Never Again

Here's the scoop. After the deluge, as per scripture, God promised He/She/It would never again wipe out the whole world, people and animals and all.

Never Again.

Never Again, I believe is what God said in Genesis. And He/She/It made this pledge to Noah, poor beleaguered and by now the very, very old Noah and to Noah's family. And by the way, the animals must have heard this pledge too, though lacking in language they may have simply ignored it as they trotted off to find forage.

Never Again. Mark well those words. I even looked them up and I quote:

Gen. 8:21-22

"Never again will I doom the earth because of man, since the devisings of man's mind are evil from his youth; nor will I ever again destroy every living being as I have done. So long as the earth endures — seedtime and harvest, cold and heat, summer and winter, day and night — shall not cease."

Well, not being one to take Torah literally, still and all, I take umbrage at the promise Never Again. Granted, I quibble. If I do not take one element literally, then why do I take this Never Again business literally? I am human is why.

So, shoot me.

I take this promise literally.

Never means never. Yet look at my world right now. Look down from my treehouse on the endless waters, tote up the casualties, both human and animal losses, and that's some broken promise. Did not God renege on that promise of Never Again? How are you/me going to believe in such a promise? Faith?

Give me a break!

Just look at the world immediately prior to The Emperor Floods. The iniquities. The corruption. The calumnies. The sufferings of the rich. The bloated plutocrats. The lying autocrats. Not to mention war, twenty-four-seven, far and wide. And that's not even counting hurricanes, tornadoes, drought, tsunami, and countless other 'agains' that doomed mankind, or, in the vernacular of political correctness, personkind.

Okay. Okay. So you observe that not every single person or creature has been wiped out 'Again.' Well, sitting in my catbird seat, how do I know whether or not every single person and animal has NOT been wiped out?

As a matter of factoid, although sea level life was/is wiped out,

I believe that those who fled uphill could not have fared much better than I have. Refugees all of them. There, they may have fled, to altitudes above how many thousands of feet? I ask you? All mashed into cramped refugee encampments, with no utilities, no food, no water. It could not have gone much better for those refugees from The Emperor Tides than for me in this treehouse. I would wager it went badly for them.

Some promise. Never Again.

And so what could God have been thinking when the promise was made to 'Never Again' launch such a punishment on evil personkind? This was a capricious act in the first place. Then to go back on the divine promise of 'Never Again', as if to say, 'Er, gee, that didn't turn out so good. Oh well, promise them anything and they will go their merry ways and still believe in Me, capital M.?'

How is one to trust such a will-o-the-wisp deity?

My Bashert

My days unfold with a regularity that includes, every single day, a few seconds of utter despair, a few minutes of heart-thumping danger, punctuated by rare moments of quiet self-reflection and long moments of, what to call it? Anesthesia.

I do not meditate. I do not pray. I am not that observant. I do, however, shout into the sky. Then, more quietly, I delve. I ponder. I remember. I reminisce. I rehash.

With nobody to corroborate my past experiences, or to offer another perspective, or to argue with my facts, or to joke me out of sinister moods, I wander, rudderless, through the detritus of my isolated memory. It is no wonder that solitary confinement was both hated and feared. And there is that word again, a derivative of solitude: solitary.

And into 'what' do I delve and ponder?

Here's an example: I had a loving husband. Dan. We were bashert. With its first two letters sounding like the first sounds that an infant can pronounce — ba ba — to its soft ending, like a whisper — hush little baby, don't you cry — shhhhhhh — bashert sounds like what it is: love and comfort and destiny.

I was his and he was mine. Really simple. For forty-three years. That was the best we could manage. And then? The inevitable.

"If you die now, Daniel Robert Steinway, I will kill you!"

"If I die now, Sarah Sacks Steinway, you won't need to!"

That was how we fought.

Don't kid yourself. Even the best husbands and wives fight. There is a way to do it and a way not to do it, and I guess our method worked because, no matter what, we stayed bashert. And we could laugh no matter what.

And so, forty-two years on, Daniel was done for.

We were informed of his bleak future in a spotless, blank little exam room at a very nice anonymous doctor's office, with virtually no eye contact throughout the pronouncement, just the sound of Danny's naked butt crinkling the immaculate white paper on the exam table.

"I am so sorry to give you this news, Mr. and Mrs. Steinway. Your tests show anomalies. We have done the very best we could possibly do. I am so sorry."

Coward.

That's how people talked back then. Even doctors. It was an era in which, everyone hedged, mouthing little niceties, like the word 'anomalies' for example, as sterile stand-ins for the real news:

"Well, sucker, it's curtains for you!"

Never say the 'D' word. So the doctor leaves the cubicle and we sit there. Couldn't he at least have waited for Danny to get dressed?

"Danny, what was that?"

"Curtains."

"Ya think?"

"Doomed," he said.

"DOOMED; all caps."

"Not so fast private Struthers."

"I always liked that one, Danny. 'Will everybody with a living mother please take one step forward.'

"Dead as a doorknob?"

"Dead meat."

"Dead letter."

"Dead tired."

"No, Daniel. It's Dog tired."

"Yeah, but it's always dead duck."

And thus, Daniel Robert Steinway was diagnosed. The word, 'diagnosed,' was the Ready-Set-Go for the corporate medical industry to shift into high gear. Diagnosis thrusts the patient and their beloveds into a medical model that marks the beginning of treatment, so-called. It was the license to poke, to prod, and to poison any poor soul who presents with certain symptoms. And the bills came tumbling in.

We fought. Not each other. The whole damn system. None of which was designed to make someone well, but most of which was designed to make someone rich. Who, you might ask? Now that is the true medical mystery.

Daniel's skin turned the loveliest shade of golden tallow. His arms, once well-muscled and useful, melted into bones, clearly delineated on the outside and pressing against his shrinking epidermis. His freckles vanished leaving his skin smooth and young.

Soon enough it was the whole damned medical industrial complex we were fighting, and not all that well. The diagnosis, with its many procedures and protocols; its appointments; its nameless doctors, nurses, staff; and pages of long-form invoices detailing tubes, and bandages, and office procedures, and going home not knowing, really, what on earth had just happened.

And so, in the end, the end of the end, it was not the bills, the prescriptions, the protocols, the appointments, of Daniel's diagnosis, but it was just us: two people who were bashert. We had to return to each other and to remember to be present in our last days in this world together before the world to come.

And so, we were silent.

We sat for unknown hours together. Sometimes, I could lie down next to him on our big bed and fall to sleep just looking at his head. Would it be now? Or now? Or now? Would I notice if he fell to sleep then fell to death? Would I wake with a jolt? Sometimes he was so quiet I had to touch his chest to see if he were still there with me. And I kissed his arm. And I did not cry except when alone in our bathroom. I cried stifled and choking, into our red terrycloth towels. He ate a banana one day. He stroked Peepers, our cat. He moved his leg across the sheet. He said to me:

"Sarah, you have your whole life ahead of you."

And then he died. Dead as a doorknob. Dead tired at the dead end of his life. Not to beat a dead horse.

By rights I should have been surviving in my treehouse here with Dan. We would have found things to laugh at together. Even the struggle would have seemed interesting. My writing about it would have taken on historic importance with Danny reading my pages each evening and encouraging me to set it all down. Just like always. And we could have started reading all these books. Reading some of them over again. Our library. Here we would have sat, surrounded by the literal warmth of our insulating books, and picking out a volume, we could have filled some of our less terrifying moments with our usual reading aloud to each other. Some of the books we would have remembered clearly as we turned the pages. Some of our previously read books we could not for a million dollars have told ourselves that we remembered reading. Weird.

Without Danny, I was loaded with memories, but fearful, too, that I would just gradually forget things, one by one, like forgetting that we had read a novel called *The Leopard*. Never again would Danny and I sit together. And pretty soon I'll be a blank, a non, and I will forget it all. Now that will be death.

A phone rings.

I am sitting on my bed in my dorm room in college, studying for an art history final. It's my senior year.

Somebody picked up.

Knocking on my door.

"It's for you. Dean Whittier."

Shit. What's that about?

"Hello, Sarah? Would you mind very much coming over to my office in a few minutes? I realize you are probably studying, but if you could take a break. Please."

Disconnect.

I walk to his office.

I had always enjoyed walking on campus after hours. The dark sycamore leaves rustling overhead. The empty sidewalks. The alumni fountain louder now that it didn't have to compete with the student pedestrians. The admin building is dark. There is a campus cop hovering at the door. His billy club reflects a glint of light from the window above the foyer. He asks me my name and, a little too unctuous I do believe, he opens the doors for me and walks me up the stairs. He's guiding me by my elbow as we walk down the silent linoleum hallway toward the dean's office. A gentleman this one. Inside the office is Dean Whittier and two men dressed in dark suits and thin ties. They stand up as I walk in.

Then we all sit down at the conference table. Coffee? No. Tea? No. Ginger ale? What, no beer? We sit there. Dean Whittier introduces the suit-men. Fat guy, Harold something-or-other, and skinny guy, Jack Sprat, I suppose. From the F. A. A.

"The what?" I ask.

Federal Aviation Administration. Dean Whittier starts the meeting by turning slightly to the skinny guy. No agenda this time. Jack Sprat reads aloud to the room from a soiled manila folder:

"NTSB Incident Identification: LAX 353471967. There has been an incident. A noncommercial pleasure and personal transport craft, Cessna 172, N 71747, en route to destination airport in Van Nuys, California, went down at or around 9:43 PM in San Bernardino County. Airplane damaged beyond repair, written off. Factors include weather, downdraft, updrafts. No record of weather briefing received by pilot. Forced landing off airport on land. Adverse and unfavorable weather. Aircraft caught in apparent updraft. Pilot attempted landing on desert road. Fuselage hit tree. cabin doors propped open Good field in range. Sky condition, clear. Visibility at accident site, unlimited. Flight plan, none. Ceiling at accident site, unlimited. Precipitation at accident site, none. Type of weather conditions, VFR."

Sprat clears his throat, gulps a squeaky bolus of snot,

"Occupants: two. Fatalities: two."

My parents were dead.

Graduation was a treat.

I called one of the boyfriends.

Hey, Dave, can I park in your life for a while? He would be the easiest. He would not demand more than just sex, and that I could handle. We would lie on the floor and I would quietly spin away. Half-stoned, numb, unthinking, half-sleeping. I dreamed I had missed my chemistry final and could not find the classroom. What did I need with chem., me, an art major?

I lived like this, in a state of torpor, in the anesthetic of stasis, for two years. And that was that: orphaned, but safe.

I worked in an art supply store.

Every day I lived with Dave, I put my sales clerk smock on, put my little shoes-ies on and off I went to work. I ended up doing this for a lifetime. A life, I made, even after leaving Dave's bed and quite in spite of my extenuating circumstances. From sales, to marketing, to advertising. I put one foot in front of the other and made a life. And then later, I made a life with Daniel Robert Steinway. My bashert.

I must stop.

Wherein I mull.

I know. This survival thing, this lone-survivor in her tree-house, gives me way too much time to think. Isn't that what I had wanted with my treehouse?

I've had fifty years to go over in my mind, the crash of my parents Cessna. I do not say 'to get over it'. And, now, after some months — years? — in my treehouse, post The Emperor Tides, I go on thinking. I think. Here's what I think:

I do not GET over things. But I mull. I consider. I think. I built my treehouse for this very purpose: to think. That is what I thought, at first. So maybe I got more thinking than I could ever have bargained for. Be careful of what you wish.

How could a skilled pilot go down under such circum-stances? Visibility, unlimited? Weather conditions, VFR?

Visual Flight Rules (VFR) are a set of regulations under

which a pilot operates an aircraft in weather conditions generally clear enough to allow the pilot to see where the aircraft is going. The pilot must be able to operate the aircraft with visual reference to the ground, and by visually avoiding obstructions and other aircraft

How, I ask myself, how could this fatal 'incident' have happened? I ask myself this question for more than fifty years. And, sitting on board my own small craft, granted it lacks flight capacity, sitting aboard my treehouse, isolated in the skies, high above endless clear horizons and with clear visual reference below me, allowing for VFR weather conditions, I have had plenty of time to think this thing out.

It's obvious. As obvious as the superb Royal Air Force pilot training that my father got during World War Two. It's as obvious as his gold wing-ed insignia. It's obvious that a Flight Sergeant would not botch mere unexpected changes in the weather.

It had to have been intentional.

The pilot had to have decided to go down. To take his craft down.

That's all.

That's it.

Obvious.

What happened in the Cessna to my father and mother?

Joe was yelling something.

"Deb. Deborah! Hands to your neck. Head to knees!"

She was so hot. So tired.

Joe yelled again.

"I'm cutting off, Deborah."

The engine roar was instantly replaced by the sound of wind tearing at the metal fuselage.

Joe, now calm, precise, and deliberate, touches each dial on the instrument panel, caressing each one with his middle finger, right hand. The finger you give the finger with. Slow down. Look carefully. See. Look at each numeral. Scan your whole mind for the correct procedure. Save your craft. Think and go slow. Listen:

"Feel the plane through your butt, Flight Sergeant Sacks! Think! Get a grip, Flight Sergeant. Think with your butt, gawdamnit Sacks, and save your men, and save your craft, and shut yer gob. and it'll all be just tickety-boo, Flight Sergeant Sacks."

Joe, slow down and think.

What could he have been thinking?

That he wanted out? That, he, the pilot — at the controls, captain of his craft, pharaonic in his powers — that he would enact a killing edict by taking his aircraft down?

And wouldn't that be the exact opposite of 'get a grip, Flight Sergeant'? You save your craft, and you save your men, and you shut yer gob? How could he have made his body do the exact opposite of what had been trained into his very synapses? What desperation could have overridden all that training? Why does anyone want to end his life plus the life of his life partner, his wife, mother of his child?

And here am I. I have turned out to be an example of the precise opposite of one who wants to end a life. I am the one, instead, who lives despite horrible circumstances. Despite extenuating circumstance. We take after our parents in ways they may never have intended. I did the opposite of mine. I have lived on and on and on despite the odds, despite the desperate odds. Am I not the exact opposite of the pilot, my father, who took the Cessna down?

And what I took away, that night in Dean Whittier's office, was that I would just keep going: on and on and on. I would.

I am drifting. It's probably the effect of too much talk. I mean typing. It's like talking. Typing. Isn't it?

I am so tired.

It must have been the birds. Talking about the birds.

I saw Daniel. He was smiling, laughing, really. One of his legs was broken with the white femur sticking out, broken into two pieces which jutted out of his torn pants leg. He was smiling and singing Bob Dylan's *Sad-Eyed Lady of the Lowlands.* And the words to the song were not being sung in Daniel's voice nor in Bob Dylan's voice. Rather, the voice sounded like the drone of a harmonium, and it could form words and sing.

Then I saw my hen house. We used to call it the Chateau Le Coop. It was built downhill from our Taliesin house. I realized that I had not fed or watered nor checked up on the hens in five years. I began to panic. I had neglected them. They would all be dead. But when I went inside the hen house, they were all right there, pecking at the feeder and drinking out of the watering chimney, and they were fat and happy, and they surged forward, the whole flock, happy to see me.

And I said in my sleep, 'I really fucked up.'

Then Daniel smiled at me and he was still singing, but I couldn't hear the song. I started to wrap a tourniquet on his leg, and I saw that the tourniquet was made out of strips of my paintings, the canvas torn along the edges, the strips thin and colorful. Then I saw that Daniel was laying on tefillin, wrapping his arm tightly, and he said to me:

"Better dead than never, Sarah."

And we laughed.

"Better dead than never, eh, Sarah?"

And I wrapped his bleeding leg in tourniquet bandages made from the torn strips of my paintings.

Then I heard talk. A woman and a man. Then I heard Daniel Robert Steinway, laughing as he laid on tefillin:

"You have your whole life ahead of you Sarah."

No Danny. My whole life is behind me now. Choose Life, they say. But here, now, I can only see that life has chosen me.

In Genesis, I read about the generous and forgiving blessing of Joseph toward his treacherous brothers.

I am afraid I am capable of no such thing.

And now, even less so, now that I have had all these decades to chew over the treachery of my pharaonic parent and his killing edict: to take the Cessna down.

Back when I decided to leave my well-shod corporate advertising self, I decided not to have children too.

Oh, perhaps it was well before that. During my interim life with Dave, immediately following the deaths of my parents, I knew that I would have been incapable of giving support to another human being of my own blood. There would have been no support, obviously, for me if I had decided to have my own children. No grandparents around to dote. No. It always seemed wiser to me not bring children into a world where their mother had no outside support.

When I met Danny, I discovered in him another form of kin —

he himself had been damaged as much as I had been perhaps, by other hard circumstances. Divorces. Deaths. Substitute dads he had had. And, Daniel, of the sad eyes, recognized in me a kindred soul. We took up nurturing one another and built our love in spite of our injured selves.

It's not as sad as it sounds. We both possessed at least some degree of elasticity. And nobody got our weird senses of humor better than we ourselves.

'If my name were Dick Peter, I'd have to change my name to Richard.'

Things like that.

See what I mean?

We healed one another, Danny and I, for more than forty years. And then we could do no more.

Sometimes you do not receive what you need from the world. You find yourself, instead, alone, hurt, angry or, less admirably, perhaps jealous. Jealous of normal people. A person like that, you might take down the whole world so that, if you could not have it, then nobody could have it. That's possible.

Without what you need, assuming it is love, or warmth, or sparkling good health, you are starting at a disadvantage. Even when you elect to pay back the world with something better than you were given, you won't quite know how to start. You're lacking a few ingredients. Or you are lacking the recipe for how to put together the meagre ingredients that you do have. You will have the devil's own time putting things to rights.

And let's say you are one of the lucky, or the bless-ed, it's unlikely, but work with me here. You are happy, healthy, mentally endowed, surrounded by more of the same by way of your parents, your siblings, your community, and let's not be coy, your race, your religion, your income, your tribe. There are so many things you need if you're to effortlessly get a leg up on life. It's unfathomable, the combination of things you need to turn out okay. Or even to turn out mediocre.

Here, up here in my treehouse, I have spun through every possible reaction to my life experiences. From desperate to terrified to starving to miserable lonesomeness to anger. And back again. Now I am maxed out. Straggling. But, as you see, still alive.

```
-VI-
Get yourself a teacher;
avoid doubt . . .


Pirke Avot 1:16
```

THE OTHER NIGHT I AM NOT SLEEPING, as usual, just lying there listening to the branches of my oak tree groaning up above my canvas roof. Bitterly, the stars are mocking. Hell, it's cold up here, and why me, and so forth, and so on. Wet. Not rain, but fog-slush, pouring around my shoulders. Shit!

And hey! You know what? I bet one of those crazy tree suits Jerry had outfitted me with would be great in the cold. Flinging stuff out of my wardrobe box, I found one. It still had its label: Every Hunter's Friend. I flung it on, one size fits all. Perfect. And there I sat. Disguised as a tree. Safe and warm. The Buddha of the treehouse.

Anyways.

The other night I hear this scratching on my tree trunk, and panting, and a kind of snarl, and I look overboard from my platform.

It's a cat! Swear to God! It's a cat. I have company.

It's a wet straggler just this side of dead, but I gotta say, he's determined, steadily climbing up the trunk of my tree. He struggles onto my platform, shakes off, and looks in my direction, aggrieved. This cat is not well pleased to find himself stranded with one of us and, knowing cats, he probably assumed that I was one of the human beings responsible for all that deep, dark water! And such a weird one indeed, I may have seemed to this cat. Who does she think she is fooling, this human one, dressed as a tree.

This cat is no fool.

Then, with a feline shrug and an assessing sniff, he gets a whiff of my bucket of Slow Fish. Trotting over to it, he peers daintily over the edge, reaches fastidiously into the bucket, and hooks one of the poor dead creatures up and into his mouth. Gulp! This activity he repeats five or six times until sated, I suppose, and then he sits down, domestic and oblivious, and sets to bathing, as cats forever are wont to do. Watching him attentively — this is my first guest in I cannot tell you how many seasons — I see that he has become a host for about a dozen enormous black ticks. They have colonized around his neck and ears and a few outliers hang from his belly like hideous black teats.

If there is one thing that has thrived after the The Emperor Tides, it is the California Black Tick. Again, evolution has been kind and swift. They are as big as a man's thumb and hearty as hell. Who wouldn't be, if you were a tick, what with all that carrion? My own experiences with these huge sucking beasties is intermittent; some have attached to me as I dipped my bucket into the waters on my forays down my stairs to gather Slow Fish. I have been meticulous about removing them. I use tweezers and it's a messy, bloody routine — a creepy bit of personal hygiene. But I figure I had better be conscientious about this task or, who knows, those ticks might suck me dry.

So, taking pity on the cat, and seeing the enormous black ticks on his face and pushing up through the long fur on his stomach, I decide to try to help him by removing some of them. Talk about squeamish. Those suckers were formidable.

Suckers! Ha! Here I am the ultimate punster and nobody's around to hear me.

Anyways.

So I reach out to the cat, and it is not a welcome gesture apparently. He bares his teeth and hisses at me mightily. I am still in my Hunter's Friend oak tree costume. Maybe this puts him off. Then he does something weird. He hoists himself up onto his hind legs, and he circles me. His front paws are raised a bit in front of his chest in an attitude, I swear, of a boxer circling his opponent in the ring, ready to throw a punch. He moves gracefully on his hind legs, with control and balance. I had never seen anything like that from a cat. I back off.

"Suit yourself, buster. It's your blood they're sucking."

His eyes stayed fastened on me. They were huge and green and wary. Then he thumped his front legs back onto the floor and resumed his catlike grooming.

As his tongue approached each tick I saw him nuzzle in tight on the base of the thing where its mouth was firmly attached to his flesh and he sucked right alongside the gripping mouth of each tick. As he did this, the size of the tick diminished like a deflating balloon.

Disgusting!

The cat repeated this methodical operation on most of the ticks until he seemed almost drunk. His eyes half shut in a cat-like inebriated torpor, he licked his lips, sighed a long purring breath, and passed out.

No kosher for this cat! And it dawned on me, as I shivered with involuntary revulsion, that the cat had learned to nourish itself by sucking the blood of the ticks. His own blood. A weird symbiosis of the ticks and the cat developed because of the cat's urgency to live. L'Chaim! Choose life! Survival of the fittest. And so it was. It was life's blood that was needed and this Draculaic cat had discovered a good source of protein. Of course, he did so out of desperation, with no idea of nourishment, probably, and perhaps he just liked the salty taste of blood. But he lived, and maybe thrived, by dining on his own blood.

As if it matters now. Who cares, I ask you?

'Who shall live and who shall die?'

Someone is approaching my treehouse. I fling off my Hunter's Friend and grab my binoculars.

It's not that it's another human being that surprises me. It's that I haven't seen one in such a very long time. God. I hope I don't have to do my pump-action-thing again!

Getting a bead on my guest, I am further surprised. It's his boat. It's not a boat, not by far, a vessel more like. As I watch him through my binoculars I see that this is no sailor. Rather, he struggles to keep himself and his vessel and a dog — he has a dog on board! — a big awkward black and now a very wet and nervous dog who is elbowing the man, looking anxiously overboard for a break in the waters to leap onto dry land. Except, of course, there is none.

Dog and man are stranded inside what I can now see, is an industrial sized mixing bowl. It is the kind of bowl, big as a Volkswagen, used in commercial kitchens, a huge rounded bowl to hold a batch of dough for 2000 cookies. Its rounded bottom makes for a very poor flotation device, but somehow the man and his dog and an oar — formed out of a wooden pizza paddle — lumber along on the choppy water. The 'oar' is the thing used to fling pizzas into hot ovens. It makes a very poor oar, too big and not big enough all at once. But somehow man and boat and dog, rock back and forth along the treacherous waters and make impossible headway. They almost go under several times as water surges athwartships. The shaky vision through my binoculars of man and mixing bowl and dog is making me seasick. There is not a chance in a million that they will make it over to my tree. I tremble, knowing that I am about to witness more death. But this dying is more urgent than the thousands of dead others I had already seen. Those deaths I had not witnessed at the moment of extremity. Now I am about to witness two souls die. They are so small. So vulnerable. But this man and this dog. That vessel. They are mine by default because I focused my binoculars on them early in their struggles and because I am paying full and mindful attention to their approaching demises. I cannot just put down my binoculars and not watch them. Therefore, they are my responsibility, inside my waterlogged heart. If I cheer them on, I also dread their deaths. As I watch through my binoculars I know, sickeningly, and it made me sick to watch them, there is not a chance that they will survive.

But chance, by nature unpredictable and chancy, favored this incompetent sailor and his nervous dog, afloat in their cooking pot and, bump, they did, into the trunk of my tree. Alive they are alive.

Remembering to welcome the strangers among you, I shout:

"Are you crazy?! This is insane! With a dog? Are you nuts!"

And so my life alone, takes another turn.

This is nuts. A man, his dog, in an industrial-sized mixing bowl. With a pizza paddle for an oar. They should have drowned.

They struggle up my stairs, thrashing and, in the case of the dog, snapping at the mighty tendrils of my loyal Praetorian Guard — my own ever-loving and slightly perverse — kudzu. They make it onto my deck, thumping, and drenched, and shaking, and splashing watery mud all over the place. The man stamps out his mud-filled shoes, pantleg flapping. He has one full pantleg and one missing pantleg. Enough fabric remains on the missing pantleg to cover his vitals, but not much more. He has a dirty white beard, the kind of beard that he may have at one time kept kempt, but now it is a short tangle of broken leaves and dripping mud. He looks around taking the measure of the treehouse, and of my disheveled self too, I suppose. He rubs one ineffectual hand down his wet beard, wringing out whatever he can. Gathering himself, and upon the completion of his ablutions, he bursts out with:

"Barukh ata Adonai eloheinu melekh ha'olam, she-hech'yanu, v'kiyemanu, v'higgianu lazman hazeh."

Immediately after this prayer of amazement at having lived to see this day, he glances over my shoulder and says:

"Oy! Hey! That's my cat!"

Pushing past me, he gathers up the cat and murmuring into its left ear he croons:

"Wally, Wally, Wally, Walliferous! Golly Wally Wallington! I thought I'd never see you this side of the world to come. You miss me? Oh Wallace, Wally, Walleye. My beautiful Wallace Barnaby Cat!"

He knows this cat?

Then, again, in thanks for making it to this day, the man repeats, rapidly this time and almost shouting:

"Barukh ata Adonai eloheinu melekh ha'olam, she-he-ch'yanu, v'kiyemanu, v'higgianu lazman hazeh."

He is nothing if not grateful, this one.

I just stand there, ineffectual. What to do? Welcome him? Pat the dog? Bring out the victuals? Are this guy and his dog Angels? Like in Torah? Meanwhile he's snuggling and crooning with the cat. Even the dog stuffs his muzzle into the cat's belly — probably with a mind to suck on the ticks, who knows.

I am starting to feel superfluous. Suddenly I am jealous. I feel stripped of my new friend, the cat. Suddenly he's somebody else's cat. Hey, it's not that easy to find friends with all this water. Here I was counting myself lucky that the cat found me. And now this. The cat is fawning over this new development on my treehouse deck. Even the dog is fawning. Everybody's fawning. Me, I'm just stupefied and envious and suddenly I'm feeling mean and low.

Here's this man, a total stranger to me, and he's an interloper between me and my cat. Well, not actually my cat, as I can plainly see. He's holding the cat like a man holding a beloved cat after a catastrophe.

Oh, please! There I go again with the puns. Sheesh. Enough already! This man's a cat person. And me, I'm stuck up a tree with a cat person and the water's rising. I weep!

Finally, he places Wallace on the deck, giving him one last, long stroke, head to tail. He looks at me and says:

"Forgive me. I quite lose myself."

"Don't mention it. I noticed."

"Let me start again. I am Mordachai Mendel. And this is Wallace Barnaby, cat among cats, and this is Laddy Labradorian, friend and boon companion. You can call me Mort. Or Rav if you must."

He extends a rather wet and grimy hand, but he has a fine handshake for a near-drowner.

"Sarah Steinway. As in piano. So, Rav it is? As in learned teacher?"

He nods.

"You are learned then?"

He shrugs, glancing away to the eastern watery horizon.

"Learned you are, but not so much these days? What with the water and all?"

He shrugs again, somber, nodding with a groan:

"Not so much these days. That is true, Sarah Steinway."

"Where did you come from?"

"Uphill. We had a little survivor's community on Mt. Tamalpais. A dozen or so stranded hikers. Boys mostly, one or two girls. And a couple of surfers who had washed up on what was left of the mountain above the waters."

"That work out okay, Rav?"

"Not so much."

Changing tack, he looks around and asks me:

"And this is where you live?"

"Yes."

"For how long?"

"Several seasons, Rabbi. Many days."

I gesture toward my makeshift calendar; knife marks and fingernail scratches along the bannister of my front porch, ten feet of weathered two-by-four. Rabbi Mort runs his fingertips lightly along the entire length of my marks.

"Oy! So many. It's hard to fathom."

It's catching, this punning germ.

"Well, Rabbi, there were some days or maybe weeks, I don't know, when I was unable, for one reason or another, to make a mark.

"Barukh ata Adonai eloheinu melekh ha'olam, she-he-ch'yanu, v'kiyemanu, v'higgianu lazman hazeh."

Again, with the grateful rabbi business. Enough already with this guy!

I suppose he's grateful for the opportunity to stay alive up here in my treehouse. I presume that he presumes that he is rescued and that he and his dog and Wallace, cat among cats, will stay up here for the duration.

"You hungry?

He looks at me, unblinking.

"What about the dog? He's hungry?

"Yes. Laddy's hungry. He has not eaten since three days, maybe four."

"Well, if he is not particular, I have fish, and I can break out a can of beans. Water, we have plenty, as you see. Clean water too. Lots of antitoxin and desal tabs.

We laugh half-heartedly. Laddy woofs.

"Barukh ata Adonai eloheinu melekh ha'olam, she-he-ch'yanu, v'kiyemanu, v'higgianu lazman hazeh."

Great! I am marooned with the King of the She-he-ch'yanus. And his dog. And, a cat among cats. Eons I spend alone and now this. I have my routines. I have my habits. I have my notions. I am my own best friend and now this. Ungrateful wretch that I am, I am not well pleased for the company.

But a hostess must rise to the occasion and must endeavor to honor her guests. I had not entertained in some time, and the circumstances of this particular event, of feeding a guest, and his dog, after cataclysmic human bungling, forces me to search way back in my upbringing for what to do. Given this extraordinary event, the arrival of these two strangers, three if we count the cat, Wallace Barnaby, I am thrust back upon my mother's training. Reminded of words so ancient as to be rendered either completely forgotten or eminently holy: Remember you were slaves in Egypt and welcome the stranger in your midst.

Or some such.

By rights, this man and his dog should have perished with all the rest of humanity. And here I am, hostess to these surviving souls, even though I myself have been left here alone to die by an unknowable God who enacts whatever He, She or It has in a His, Her or It's greater plan. I am a tiny bit curious to see how this all plays out.

But first, to eat.

I spread out the Bekins moving blanket on the floor and fetch some cans of beans, a pail of my finest Slow Fish, some canned olives, and a much-depleted bottle of Chateau Lafitte. Laddy is deeply interested in the bucket contents and sticks his long snout right down among the fish and starts to slurp. Poor thing. Wally sits by, in shocked feline disdain, at this rough character. Cats would never be so crass as to actually act hungry.

Rav Mendel and I sit down on the blanket; legs crossed like campers at a sleepover and I set to organizing the picnic. Moving cans and contents a little to the left, a little to the right. Placing my utensils — forks, spoons, and couple of steak knives — pushing them a bit in this direction, a bit in that direction, and moving the small objects — salt cellar, candle glass, a serving spoon — to make a welcoming table for my guests.

I am holding the bottle of Lafitte on my lap. Rav Mendel nods in my direction:

"May I?"

"Yes, of course, rabbi."

"Baruch… atah… Adonai…"

He takes it very slowly, very deliberately, this time, infusing each syllable with intensity, his eyes squeezed shut. Thin tears leak from his eyelids and drizzle down his cheekbones. He continues the prayer:

"Eloheinu… Melech… Ha'olam,…"

It is a sound so far back in my memory as to be nearly lost, yet I hear it so clearly in Rav Mendel's slow cadence:

"borei… p'ri… hagafen."

He holds the wine bottle with both hands, and raises it in front of his face, and studies it carefully, as if he were examining an ancient object that had been recently dug up from an anthropological site in the Sinai. He then raises it to his lips and sips, holding the liquid the way a wine connoisseur would hold a mouthful of something golden and fine, the better to perceive its subtlety, its fruit, its effect as it sloshes around the taste buds. And he swallows:

"Ahhhhh."

He hands the bottle, precious and bless-ed, back to me, and I hold it in my lap for a moment. Time has slowed. I am deaf, with a ringing in my ears. Big blobs of blindness float across my field of vision. Since my illness, this happens. Still. I take a small sip and sit holding the bottle in both hands between my knees.

"You are alive, Sarah Steinway."

"Yes. Alive. Yes."

"Cheers! L'chaim."

He lifts his chin in my direction, signaling for the wine bottle.

I just sit there looking across the blue quilted Bekins blanket at the little rabbi. My vision clears enough to focus on him. This is the first time I've really looked at him. And he is quite small, really. The kind of skinny that implies very great tensile strength of the bones and surprising reserves of stamina. If you are running a three-legged race, always pick for your partner one of these small bony types, and you will always cross the finish line first.

"And so, this is your karma, Sarah Steinway."

"That doesn't sound very rabbinic, Rav."

"On the contrary. I've had a conversation or two with the yogis."

He sits for a moment, then gestures with a little four-fin-gered, palm upward wave, indicating for me to hand him the bottle back. I reach across the blanket and hand it to him. He holds it, again, like an object reincarnated from ancient times. He rubs the somewhat smudged label with his thumb and starts to read the script of the logotype and all the tiny informational bits, word by word, aloud, but gently, savoring the tiny typeface. He reads carefully the date of the vintage. The date is the only item on the label that he takes some private issue with, and he looks over at me, eyebrows raised. It is either in astonishment over how fine a wine this is or astonishment at what bilge water it is. I can't tell. It's been so long since I needed to read a person's face to detect feelings that are not articulated.

"Karma, Sarah Steinway, is all the stuff that happens to a person."

This is weird. First, that another person is sitting here with me. Second, that he is a rabbi. Third, that we are dining on Slow Fish and canned beans, and Chateau Lafitte. Fourth, that, when you think about it, the population in my neck of the woods has just doubled — quadrupled if you count Laddy and Wallace Barnaby. It's too much to take in. So, fifth, this little rabbi starts talking about karma. It's more than a girl can take.

Rav Mendel takes another slow, appreciative sip of the wine. There is something comic, yet off-putting, about seeing a deso-late man sipping directly from a bottle of Chateau Lafitte. But he adds to the gesture such a pantomime of delicacy and fine man-ners that some of the imagery of being down and out disappears, and he is simply a rabbi blessing the wine in an ancient cere-mony of gratitude.

"The hard part, Sarah, comes after all the stuff that happens to you."

"I don't follow you, rabbi."

"It's what you do afterward, after all the stuff that happens to you, that counts. Ever read Viktor Frankl?"

"Oh, sure, yes, well, ages ago, college maybe."

"Well, then you already know, Sarah, that the problem with philosophers is too many words and very few illustrations. You are an artist, no? And so you might have preferred pictures, sketches, and the like. But you may perhaps also recall that Frankl's prime assertion was this: it's what you do after the shit hits the fan that separates the sheep from the goats — if you don't mind my mixed metaphors."

Another sip on the wine and Rav Mendel continues:

"Now Viktor Frankl must have been born with a very sunny disposition. A thread of optimism must have wound throughout his DNA. Basically, it's what you do with your catastrophes that counts. We all experience bad things. Frankl's view is that, if we can come out on the other side, we have the option to make something positive out of even the horrors. Frankl walked out of Auschwitz and created an entire psychology of survival — so to speak — and built an institute dedicated to the study of survival. I like him very much, Sarah."

What? Was I hallucinating? I am so confused. Is this a dream?

"You have, apparently, Sarah Steinway..."

"Please, just call me Sarah."

"So. Sarah, yes. You have survived perhaps the greatest human cataclysm ever to have taken place in history. Only it's unlikely to make it into history as there's virtually nobody around to remember it or care. Except you, of course. But that's asking too much, really."

I cannot cope. This is too much to take in. I need to lie down. Rav Mendel continues:

"And that's where your dharma kicks in."

This is way too much. I do not understand a word this man is saying. What's he talking, with karma and dharma? It's crazy, this talking!

"Are you crazy? This is insane! What are you saying, rabbi?"

I tumble over onto my side and curl into a fetal position. I am minding my own treehouse business when this man, his dog, and earlier his cat, show up, and he starts crazy-talking about karma, and drinking my wine, and eating my Slow Fish. I am going crazy. I am done for. I am out of the practice of intelligent conversation and for learned discourse over wine and dinner. I close my eyes and hope to sleep, and listen to Rav Mendel as he waxes crazy:

"From Wikipedia, and I quote, Sarah Steinway, quote: In certain contexts, 'dharma' designates human behaviors considered necessary for order of things in the universe, principles that prevent chaos, behaviors and action necessary to all life in nature, society, family, as well as at the individual level. Dharma encompasses ideas such as duty, rights, character, vocation, religion, customs, and all behavior considered appropriate, correct, or morally upright... numerous definitions of the word dharma, such as that which is established or firm, a steadfast decree, statute, law, practice, custom, duty, right, justice, virtue..."

"Rabbi! I can't take it anymore!"

He takes up where he left off:

"… morality, ethics, religion, religious merit, good works, nature, character, quality, property. Yet, each of these definitions is incomplete, while a combination of these translations do not convey the total sense of the word dharma. In common parlance, dharma means 'right way of living' and 'path of righteousness'." Unquote, Wikipedia."

"What's with the punctiliousness about giving credit to Wikipedia, Rabbi? I mean, it's long gone, dead. Who's to care? And, as for your 'right way of living, well, Rabbi, in case you hadn't noticed: before The Emperor Flood, that dusty concept bit the dust, er, not to harp."

Then I drop like a stone into a dream-cluttered sleep.

A few days later, we sit across from one another, legs crossed, dinner companions again. We passed between us a bottle of Pomerol 2012 from Chateau Gombaude-Guillot. Not having wine glasses, we opted for chugging straight from the bottle again. Yet, as I had earlier observed, Rabbi Mort managed to imbue our drinking with a flair for the elegant, and at each sip, he gazed long and concentrated at the label, reading carefully every word even down to the warnings.

"Already quite approachable, Mrs. Steinway. I am given to understand that this wine could last an additional twenty years or more."

"Sarah. Really, Rabbi. Call me Sarah."

"Alright. Sarah."

"You seem to appreciate your wine, Rabbi."

"That's a truism. Sarah. Yes, I like my wine. Yet, I do not tipple in the minor leagues. No, no, no. That would be an affront to, well, to God, wouldn't it?"

"Now you've lost me, Rabbi."

Well, I suppose it was his tradecraft after all — his talking of God, whoever He, She or It might be. After all he was in the God business. And what did I know? Worse. How much could I tolerate in after-dinner conversation about God? Wine, yes. I could talk of wine. Or books. Or birds. At least I used to be able to carry on those kinds of harmless dinner gambits. But water and survival had taken their tolls on my patience. What was the point of chat? Especially about religion.

"Well, Sarah, as I say, this Pomerol is quite fine. And how many years has it been sequestered in your wine cellar? Or should I say, in your wine treehouse? Not, I would posit, in the best of conditions, the most salubrious of conditions, for the preservation of any fine wine."

He took another gentle pull.

"Yet, it is still a fine, a most credible drink."

"Rabbi?"

"Yes."

"Can you tell me how you come to be sitting here commenting on my wine storage?"

He looked away and stared, eyes half closed, looking east as the sun set somewhere behind my treehouse. The oak branches darkened into silhouettes and hung down like long arms as if to embrace us.

"My first posting as a rabbi was to India. In a town called Kerala. Did you know that there is an ancient branch of Judaism on that big continent? People in that community believe, or say that they believe, that their forebears fled eastward sometime after the destruction of the second temple. I found their stories to be fascinating and profoundly touching. They had carried on their outer practices of their Jewish heritage without having much contact with any other Jews for many generations. Yet they persevered. If their observances were tilted slightly from the norm, I still admired their tenacity. They were truly holy souls. You see?"

While I could grasp what he was telling me, I am not sure that I felt any kindred connection to these far-off ancestors. The distance between an American secular Jew and an Indian Jew who clings to Judaism is more than just thousands of miles. If they are holy, what would that make me? As if hearing my thoughts, Rabbi Mort said:

"It's hard to imagine the necessity, the intensity, what should I call it? The absurdity, even? The tenacity of an isolated branch of Jewish cousins to carry on against the odds of sheer time and space that threatened to damage or to completely wipe out their belief system. As I say. They were holy."

"So then what function did you serve, Rabbi?"

"I served there as a student. These people did not require classes introducing them to their heritage. I felt I had more to learn from them than I had to teach them. And so, I hiked into the nearby, less inhabited landscape, to seek a teacher. I found him sitting in front of a very makeshift little home, a structure made of boxes, made of string. Not unlike the structures we used to see before the flood, the homes of the homeless I am remembering now, Sarah."

He paused a very long time. I thought he might have fallen asleep. Yet he snapped to attention and continued his story.

"My teacher told me he was named B.KS. Patel. The initials were for Brahma. Krishna. Shiva. And Patel was his family name. But he instructed me to call him Ramanand, his teacher's name whom he had revered, and so he used that name, late in his own life, as a kind of nom de meditation. He was very old he told me, in the final phase of life, although he was so slender and so smoothly muscled that I could not tell, in reality, how old he might have been. He told me he was a yogi. In the beginning, I had no concept of what he could have meant by the word 'yogi.' If he were part of the Jewish community in Kerala, I never discovered. But he and I began to talk and, while talking, he would gently place his limbs into various shapes and then he would settle with grace, ease and comfort as we chatted. I soon learned, without him saying so to me, that I should imitate his postures as we spoke. Sort of monkey-see-monkey-do. You see?"

As he told me about his teacher, Rabbi Mort shifted twice into seated poses of much grace and elegance. Then he continued:

"The poses served to settle my mind, and I could listen with very great care and consciousness to what Ramanand was teaching. If I may digress a bit here Sarah... Do you remember how it was before The Emperor Tides when so many people were taking yoga lessons and so many people were meditating and creating mindfulness? And do you remember that so many other people were making chaos, shooting people, blowing up people — including total strangers — and killing and maiming passersby in the most random and therefore frightening ways? I observed, back then, before the water wiped it all away, that there were two 'camps', for lack of a better word, two opposing humanities — one brutal and irrational and horrific and the other group turning quietly inward, thus separating themselves from the brutality of the other camp. Oh, and vice versa too. The brutalists were turning away from the contemplatives. Simultaneously, these two worlds of humanity had developed, as if one gave birth to the other. Yin and yang, I suppose you could say, although those are kind of woo-woo words for labeling the intrinsic powers of those two opposing humanities."

"Well, Rabbi, I must have turned into a kind of hybrid of those two types. I mean. With the life I have been forced to live, in order to survive, I use elements of both those types."

He looked at me with his attentive, hooded eyes and said nothing.

"I mean Rav, I do what I have to in order to survive. It's no joke. I don't think any one of us is all one thing or all the other."

"You then believe, Sarah, in moral relativity?"

"Suit yourself, Rabbi."

"Yes? Sarah?"

"Look, Rabbi. I have had to commit heinous acts — and I do mean this in the plural — I have committed premeditated murder to keep myself alive. It's no picnic out here, Rabbi. And you quibble about my believing in 'moral relativity'. Feh! I'm doing the best I can. At least I notice it when I commit my rationalization for my immoral acts."

I twisted away from him on our blanket. I was so tired.

The next morning, I wake up to the sunrise, and it beams in on me all glorious and affecting, and I think for a moment that I am waking up in my Taliesin house after having slept in the living room on the sofa. But there is an odd moving shadow casting here and there, and I realize I am still living in my treehouse and that it is Rav Mendel, out on the deck, doing triangle pose.

Oh, for heaven's sake!

This is preposterous.

"Rabbi! What are you doing?"

"Good morning, Sarah Steinway."

He shifts, rotating his torso in a twist, ribcage up and forward. He is making a revolved triangle, moving slow and effortlessly, and I must say, he does this with superb ease, comfort, and stability. One pantleg is still intact, the other, missing, revealing long, thin, well-muscled quadriceps. His lower hand is thin and long-fingered and tanned into leather and it is made up of tendons rising and pushing into the covering flesh, and the veins are blue, and they are delineated clearly on the back of his hand, which supports his pose.

I cannot believe it, that hand, a hand probably accustomed to holding sacred objects: a Torah scroll, a yod with its likeness of a pointing hand. His hand beneath his triangle pose is as beautiful as it would be holding that pointing instrument, that little silver hand. His hand is that kind of hand, and now it supports the whole edifice of his triangle pose.

"I noticed your rolled-up yoga mat, Sarah. I hope you are not offended."

"Be my guest. I mean no harm; after all, you are my guest."

"Good. Well, since I am your guest, I think perhaps I must

give you a gift of some sort. I would ordinarily want to bring something, a token, to warm the house of my host, like the standard bouquet of flowers, or a little book of verse, or a whole cherry pie. At this point, I am obliged to be more creative with my offering. And so, I propose, to give you the gift of a few moments of guided yoga practice. I cannot have helped but notice that this yoga mat was very dusty, and it had been so tightly rolled for such a long period of time that it was very hard to spread out flat. Would you accept my offering of a few moments of guided yoga practice as a hostess gift?"

"Well, rabbi, I've been busy just staying alive."

"All the more so to do a bit of yoga each day. You are not into yoga then, Sarah?"

This is really annoying. Out of nowhere, this man, this supposed rabbi, floats into my life and already he is chiding me for not doing enough yoga? A rabbi, no less? What the heck's going on here? Maybe I'm getting sick again.

Elvis?

"Well, Sarah? Yoga makes you strong."

"I am strong already, Rabbi."

"Yes, I can see that. Oh well then. Suit yourself, Sarah, but do you mind if I complete my practice?"

"Suit YOUR-self, rabbi."

I am sulking.

Am I sulking?

Nothing like infrequent human interaction to ruin a girl's whole day. I was doing fine before this interruption. I sit on the floor, cross-legged, slumped at the waist, and I watch as Rav Mendel continues his program.

He moves slowly. He holds each pose for a long while. I see him make a downward dog by using his forearms instead of his hands out in front.

"This, Sarah Steinway, is what I call Cubit Dog. It is the embodiment of the ubiquitous cubit found in Torah. As you already know Sarah, a cubit is the distance from the middle finger to the elbow, and it was a measuring device for many projects described in Torah. Thus, it makes the ideal measurement for a very strong downward dog. You like?"

"Ingenious, Rabbi."

It was going to be a long day.

"You know, Sarah. We Jews have a history of embodying our Jewishness. Look at davening and shuckeling for instance."

I do not like being lectured. He is losing me.

"Rabbi, I have a million things to do. Every day I have a million things to do. Collect and/or concoct fresh water. Rinse out the outgoing bucket. Catch Slow Fish. Cut back the kudzu. Tidy up myself and my quarters. And now I have guests so that means more fish and water needed, and more outgoing, if you get my drift. I'm busy."

"I am so sorry, Sarah. I have been rude. Can I help? Aside from my yoga and my prayers, I am really quite handy around the house. Please. Let me help."

He thumps soundlessly down from his headstand.

We spend the rest of the day performing all of the routine tasks that comprise my having been a sole-survivor. Now I have a worthy assistant. I discovered early on that if I do not keep up with processing water, collecting fish, and keeping clean, that things get out of hand, and I endanger myself to the point where

I could starve and, once on that path, I would lose the energy and the will-power to continue. I would surely die. Not that at times I have not actually desired to die. But generally, I do prefer to live and so I keep up my schedule of tasks. You could say I am religious about house-keeping.

Even this written record of my life takes time, and it has to fit it into my schedule. Barring threats such as bad weather, or illness, or a change in the tides, or an increase in the quantities of carrion and trash floating by — necessitating my shoving it off my tree trunk or the first few steps of my stairs — or just plain old lonesome depression, I try to write every day.

I show Rav Mendel the ropes, and we work until the late afternoon. I show him how to make a mark on my front porch rail to count the days I have been here. Then we sit down, and I show him my typewriter and my waterproof briefcase with pages of writing. It's not well organized. I suffer for lack of an editor. But mox nix. He starts to read. And then he places his beautiful and slender and strong yogic hands on the keyboard and he types:

After some time, several seasons I do believe, the situation on Mount Tamalpais had reached such a pass that I was moved to bury my tefillin and my Torah scroll. To put them to rest in safe hiding under the earth, was to save my own life. A mitzvah. It was to be the burial of sacred objects, exactly as we do when a Torah scroll is damaged beyond repair. In this case, the burial of sacred objects would serve to save my own life. It was my very life that would soon be beyond repair if I did not act. In an increasingly dangerous situation, my Torah had to go into hiding as I would soon also need to do.

The kids — they had been hiking when a huge tide came in and did not recede and, instead, made of Mount Tam an island — those kids, mostly boys and a couple of girls, became savages. They had cut thick tree branches, swinging them for cudgels and they swung these armaments at any one or any thing that raised their blood. Failing to feed their bellies adequately, they fed their hatreds instead — the usual grudges against anyone not of their own tribe, or color, or creed. They made clothing out of tree bark and the occasional fur from a bludgeoned animal. They ate those creatures raw, tearing at bloody entrails and fighting off one another in violent free-for-alls that often resulted in crippling injuries and subsequent deaths. They danced, and they did howl. The kids also fished as best they could, leaning towards the treacherous tides with hands cupped, grabbing whatever fish they could without sliding down the slopes of Mt. Tam, which now formed steep and rocky beaches. One or two lads went into the sea. I did what I could to recite the Kaddish, but that act infuriated my companions and I realized my act endangered my very life. That is when I decided to find a hiding place.

I escaped the instability of the youths by hiding in the topmost crags of Mt. Tam with my cat and dog. For a while we subsisted on fern fiddleheads and the cat was adept at hunting, so, too, the dog. And both were more skilled and gracious with their prey than the human beings down below had been.

I laid to rest the objects of my identity in a deep fragrant earthen pit lined with ferns. I marked the place well in my field of vision, triangulating on several distant objects: a boulder, an arroyo, and the distant topmost peak of Mount Diablo. Thus, inscribed upon my mind's eye, was the place where I had consecrated the burial of my most holy self. I hoped I would be able to retrieve those objects after... well... after whatever this was... was over.

That is my story: may their memory be a blessing and may I find these objects again, alive and holy, at some future date.

Signed, Rabbi Mordechai Mendel

And then we spied a raft. Actually, we heard it first, the ear-splitting wail of a very worn outboard motor, alarming us as we set to our chores — man-made sounds being all the more jarring after years of not hearing anything.

We — Rav Mendel, Laddy, Wallace Barnaby, and I — we all turned in unison to the sound of a motor-driven vehicle in the near distance.

Oh, for God sakes!

It was a raft with a woman at the tiller, and a tent pitched on the boards, and a neat stack of boxes. The raft had an outboard motor, and six more outboard motors were lined up side by side on the deck, and this woman and her vessel were making good time across the now pretty low tidal waters. When she got right under my tree, I looked down at her and she yelled up at me:

"Anybody up there?"

And I shouted back:

"Nobody but us hallucinations."

To which she guffawed, belly and throat, and she yelled up to me:

"Permission to come aboard."

And I grudgingly granted her permission.

"How do I get up there?"

"Poke around in the kudzu and you'll find stairs. And a handrail. Careful of the tendrils on that vine. It'll grab you if you hesitate more than a millisecond. That vine is strong, and wily, and needs watching, or it'll make a meal of any person or animal who can't move fast enough to get past its greedy grasp. Come on up if you can. Don't blame me if you can't."

"Aye, aye captain!"

Down below I watch her as she thrusts a long boathook at my lower steps and she hauls the barge close in, snug. She fastens the boat with an impressive and stout set of sailor's knots. This woman is as seaworthy as her vessel. My inimitable kudzu leans in twirling a few tendrils around the rope and she hacks them back, workmanlike and strong. It's love/hate with that vine. She gives it a withering glare and it shrinks back, subservient for the moment. She shouts up at me:

"Ya gotta be firm with kudzu. But once it knows who's boss, it's as loyal as some husbands."

Kudzu. Another example of how evolution has speeded up the invention of new species. My kudzu — a product of ample garbage and unfettered opportunity — grows so fast and is so voracious it serves as a guardian angel to my lair. So long as I keep it cut back, which has become a daily ritual, another chore so to speak, every morning, then I can get up and down the steps myself on my forays into the low tidal waters to get my ration of Slow Fish. We have a symbiotic relationship, that vine and I. Symbiosis seems to be the watchword of these times. My new visitor seems to have already had much experience with kudzu. She gives it no quarter.

Boat woman is no coward. She bounds up, whacking off dozens of grasping tendrils with effective blows. Before I am completely ready for another guest, she's on board, hand extended in bon ami.

"Zelda Wurlitzer, Rabbi Emerita!"

She grabs my hand in a powerful handshake, her fingers raspy, and nicked, and bleeding from dozens of tiny abrasions. She cranes to look up into my face. I am taller than she by a foot. She wears large coke-bottom glasses — unbroken, miracle of miracles — and booms as she pumps my hand, my whole arm for that matter.

"And you are?"

"Sarah Steinway. As in piano."

"So! We have an organ and a piano!"

Then suddenly, Zelda bounds forward, grabbing Rav Mendel.

"Morty!"

She's engulfs him in such a powerful embrace that his feet leave the floor. She bellows over his shoulder, oblivious to his hanging legs:

"Mort and I go way back. Don't we Morty?"

"Zel! Zeldy, Zeller, Zellinsky. Beautiful Zelda Wurlitzer."

What's with this guy? For a learned rabbi, he certainly hyperbolizes the hyperbole. Zelda puffs up,

"We, dear Sarah Steinway, as in piano, go way back."

All the way into pre-history, I am about to discover.

Seems that Rabbi Zelda Wurlitzer and Rav Mordechai Mendel were major minor collaborators doing Biblio-Drama, song and dance numbers, as opening acts for the stars during the sixties at rock concerts. Billed as:

The Rockin' Rabbis, Rock-Solid Torah for Rock 'n Rollers.' They were huge in a small-time sort of way. Sort of like a Jefferson Putt-Putt to the Jefferson Airplane.

Rav Mort — duly deposited back onto his own two feet — beams at Zelda as she surges toward me:

"May I hug you?"

"Me? Why?"

"Because, darling girl, there are not that many people left to hug. And I like to hug. And because, I am still alive. And apparently you are too. And Morty, and Wallace, and Laddy. And it's been a long and winding road. I can tell you. And I am miserable. And, oh, for God's-sake. Give us a hug!"

Zelda is a hugging fool. She hugs me. Hugs Morty again. Hugs Wallace Barnaby. Hugs Laddy. Then starts all over again, hugging us all in an enormous group hug. You can't help laughing. And then we are crying.

Poor me.

Poor us.

Poor world.

Suddenly and rapturously, Rav Mort launches into:

"Barukh ata Adonai eloheinu melekh ha'olam, she-he-ch'yanu, v'kiyemanu, v'higgianu lazman..."

I interrupt,

"Look Mort. Zelda. I get that you are both grateful for this impromptu reunion and for my treehouse being out here in the middle of nowheres." Mort interrupts:

"We could not have missed it. Your treehouse. I mean. The paintings. I could see them for miles and miles."

"Me, too, Mort. I headed right for them after I left Mount Diablo."

This was getting interesting. I wanted to hear more:

"You came from Mount Diablo, Zelda?"

"Yes."

"How many others were out there? Did you all form a community? Were people helpful? Did they help one another? Did you have enough to eat?"

Silence. Zelda sagged a bit.

"Not so much, Sarah-la. But I will say this: both Mort and I are very grateful for finding you. Someone like you. It's not been easy. We are so very grateful for your hospitality."

We needed levity. It had been so long since I had cracked a joke or made a wisecrack. But the chill in the atmosphere was palpable. I waded in:

"Let's eat! Unless we get to it and eat, we'll all be nothing but the Grateful Dead. So enough, already, Mort, with your she-he-ch'yanus. Let's just posit that God, He, She or It, will know in His, Her or It's heart, that we are all grateful and leave off with the constant lengthy praying business. Okay?"

Mort and Zelda are crestfallen. I see them exchange a little look between themselves. And they turn their attention back to me with just a flicker of a smile on Zelda's lips. I continue:

"I mean no criticism, rabbis."

They brighten a notch.

"But you see…"

Interrupting, Mort says:

"Of course, Sarah. Of course. Of course. Of course. It's a logical assumption that a God such as ours, that He, She or It, would take it for granted that we, bedraggled and surviving and ever and…"

He drifts off.

You see what I mean?

One minute alone, desperate, and serving my life's sentence. Next minute, surrounded by company, noise, and confusion, a regular performing troupe they are. And they're olden pals to boot. Seventy-five years I'm a secular Jew, and nary a rabbi crosses my threshold. Now, suddenly, I'm all chock-a-block with rabbis. Oy!

-VII-
It is not up to you
to finish the work.
Yet:
You are not free to avoid it.

Pirke Avot 2:16

AND SARAH LAUGHED.

Well, of course she did. Remember her? The Sarah in Torah?

Remember when she was told she would bear a child at somewhere around ninety years of age; what else could she have done? It seemed ridiculous to her.

It occurs to me that the same could have been said for my treehouse project at my rather advanced age of seventy-five. And, not unlike my ancient namesake, Sarah, I could have, and perhaps should have, laughed too. Yet, as it turns out, this treehouse has been my baby.

Not unlike with a child, my treehouse and I have passed various milestones over the past several seasons. There was the anticipation of its birth. There was the labor at its birthing. There were its first steps. It began to speak. There has been illness. Even a wicked witch, or two, has threatened it. Protective as a mother, I learned that anybody who messed with my baby was dead.

I love this baby.

Now, just in time, my baby is to be 'socialized'. We have company. Two human beings and two animals. Time for my treehouse to experience empathy, to learn how to communicate with others in meaningful ways. Socialization may be a difficult passage for my baby. After all, I have been alone for a very long time. I'm a veritable hermit. I have my ways of doing things. I live a busy life. In fact, I survive by having my routines in place. This transition to being a part of human society may put a strain on my baby, my treehouse. Not to mention: on me.

So, let's see how this goes.

The two rabbis, Zelda and Mort, are with me for five more weeks. I divided up the housekeeping tasks and gave each of them things to do that related to their particular skills. Zelda prepared and cooked our meals and cleaned up after. She also tended the 'pot' gardens and there was a nice harvest of pole beans to inspire her soups. Mort was very good at catching Slow Fish. And being very nimble, he could race up and down to the roof to repair the water catching device and collect the bottles of fresh fog-water. He mended nails in the building that had started to pop out of the wood with years of expansion and contraction. He had a good eye for spotting things in the building that needed repair, and he was inventive in making do with very little in the way of tools and patches. And he cleaned, and swept, and polished, and spit-shined everything inside and out.

Even the animals, Laddy and Wallace Barnaby, added to the conviviality of my little home. Laddy would pad around to each of us in turn, nudging his snout, nosey, into whatever we were working on, stepping on our toes, and uttering the occasional soft woof.

Wallace Barnaby slept a lot as all cats do, but he also acted as sentinel of sorts. He would stroll out to the east deck and scan the horizon, all the while standing on his hind legs, quite upright and steady, looking for all the world like a human man, hands in pockets. He would stand there, scanning the water, seeing whatever cats can see that we cannot see.

I cleaned the outgoing buckets, a job that had grown exponentially since the guests had arrived and which needed to be attended to several times each day. I also went through all of the storage containers and reorganized my supplies and equipment. The first aid box was in sorrowful disarray. Then I sorted my scant wardrobe and consigned some pieces of my clothing to cleaning rags. Over the years I had also collected a hodge-podge of useful items that had floated by, and I reviewed these objects, and categorized them, and placed them in various storage boxes. What a melancholy little chore. I had a pile of lost items from our vanished suburb. Lengths of string, buttons, plastic spoons, little jars, ballpoint pens, a rake, a brand-new Firestone truck tire, a red silk scarf, and most significantly, my cowboy — girl, girl — my cowgirl hat, a Stetson, almost new. What a waste it would have been to let it go out to sea, still sitting at a jaunty angle on a passing corpse.

I'm like that. Thrifty.

At the end of our workdays, we would each take a turn at the typewriter, then dinner and talk.

The sun, reliable orb, was each day appearing to move farther south, and after a couple of weeks, it was setting south of the distant island of Mount Diablo.

"Have you given any thought to observing the High Holy Days, Sarah?"

"You are joking, right, Zelda?"

"On the contrary. These traditions can provide solace, especially in extreme circumstances. Mort and I could cobble together a series of services. Do a bit of singing, read from Torah, develop a theme for this year's observances, deliver a sermon. It's no bother. We estimate that it might be Rosh Hashanah by now and Yom Kippur to follow in a week's time. You up for it Sarah?"

"Oh sure. A fast. A feast. As you see Rabbi Zelda, out here feast and fast are mostly the same thing. So what's your theme this season?"

"Scapegoats."

"Perfect. Ideal. Plenty of those to go around these days."

I could see how scapegoats fit, considering our circumstances right now. The sermon should make quite a splash.

Sorry. Really. I need a twelve-step program for my addiction to water-based puns. My name is Sarah, and I am a punster.

Three days later we gathered to celebrate the new year. L'shanah tovah! We were a tiny congregation, heavy on the rabbinic component. But Laddy and Wallace Barnaby filled in the pews.

Reading aloud from *The Torah: A Women's Commentary* by Eskenazi and Weiss, Mort started with the narrative:

"Aaron shall take two he-goats and let them stand before the Lord at the entrance of the Tent of Meeting; and he shall place lots upon the two goats, one marked for the Lord and the other marked for Azazel."

I interrupt:

"You mean to say, Rabbi, that this was a lottery so to speak? That the life or death of the two goats rested upon the flip of a coin?"

Mort looked me in the eye, long and unblinking, and continued:

"Aaron shall bring forward the goat designated for the Lord, which he is to offer as the purgation offering; while the goat designated by lot for Azazel shall be left standing alive before the Lord, to make expiation with it and to send it off into the wilderness of Azazel."

Zelda continued reading commentary from *The Torah: A Women's Commentary* by Eskenazi and Weiss:

"Azazel is the name of the wilderness beyond the boundaries of settled life... Azazel is best imagined as a place of disorder."

I interrupt:

"Like here, huh, Zelda?"

Zelda fastens me with another long rabbinic gaze. She had the kind of expression that an exasperated parent gives to a toddler. She continued her reading:

"The scapegoat effectively conveys the chaotic aspects of human life back to a place of origin."

Mort continued reading the service from our copy of the Torah:

"The live goat shall be brought forward. Aaron shall lay both his hands upon the head of the live goat and confess over it all the iniquities and transgressions... putting them on the head of the goat: and it shall be sent off to the wilderness. Thus, the goat shall carry on it all the iniquities to an inaccessible region;

and the goat shall be set free in the wilderness."

I interrupt:

"So, rabbis. Are we like those goats? We carry the sins of our tribe on our heads? And off we get sent into the wilderness, this wilderness of flood? Is that your point, Rabbis?"

They are silent. I continue:

"We are the scapegoats shoved off into the chaotic lands? To expiate the sins of our kind? To sort of make up for us experiencing any of that thing called 'survivor guilt'?"

No response. Onward I go:

"And later on, instead of an actual animal, a word — the word 'scapegoat' — evolved, and whoever was burdened with the mere word, was to take the blame for whatever sins or wrongs that occurred in a more civilized world. So-called. But of course, it was not a civilized world at all, was it? Just a world where certain people were named as scapegoats. But, not unlike those original animal goats, the human scapegoats were also tossed into the wilderness of Azazel. Then what?"

Rabbi Mort and Rabbi Zelda, were, by now, listening with some attention.

I warm to my commentary:

"I mean. I mean to say, rabbis, then what happened? 'Then what' is always the next question. So, after leaving Egypt, 'then what?' So after the tablets 'then what?' So after Moses died, 'then what?' That is our most important question. Whether secular or observant, the next question is always 'then what?' You said it yourself, quoting Frankl. It's what you do after the shit hits the fan that counts. The dharma part. Then what are you going to do. Right Rav Mort?

"So we name the scapegoat, or goats, and the human scape-goat bears the iniquities of the world. And the one who is named 'scapegoat' gets all the blame for the sins of the world. Is that right, rabbis?"

They nodded. I continued:

"And that person, the human 'scapegoat' is expected to expiate all the guilt of humankind and is expected to walk with a meek and self-deprecating slump so that the casual observer will know who to point the finger of blame at the next time there is a blameworthy event.

"I doubt that any human scapegoat, in our modern era and using our politically correct terminology, has had as much to look forward to as those animals, those actual goats, who survived during ancient ceremonies of expiation when shoved into the wilderness of Azazel."

I stopped to take a breath.

I do not think that my rabbi guests were very happy about my long-winded exegesis on the word 'scapegoat'. But they were patient with me. On I went:

"So, let's review some of the many scapegoats who got tapped with blame and were tagged as responsible for the sins and inequities of The Emperor Floods. Shall we? Yes?:

The Leader, cap 'L'.

The Congress.

The communists.

The terrorists.

Pollution.

The moon — poor moon — made it happen.

Rising tides, melting north polar ice.

Or was that southern polar ice?

Climate change did it? Nonsense! No such thing. No scapegoat there.

Human evil did it — greed, lust, sloth, envy.

Meteors from outer space did it.

Aliens — you name their origins — Mars, Pluto, Mexico? did it.

Stupid old Darwin?

Stupid old Chevron?

Stupid old CIA?

"And on and on it went. Yes, rabbis? We had no end of scapegoats as The Emperor Floods advanced. And then you know what happened? Well, you do, after all, you do know.

"Litigation. Every 'thing' and every 'one' who landed on a scapegoat list was sued. Sued, they were, in every court in the land: civil, federal and municipal, all the way right up to the Supreme Court of the land. Lawsuits. Lawsuits. Lawsuits. Day and night. Am I right, Rabbis?"

They are silent. Numb? And I continue:

"Whatever happened to 'Justice, Justice shall you pursue?'

"But I see now that we could posit that we here, I, Sarah Steinway, and her guests in her treehouse — two rabbis, a dog, a cat — I can see how we might be labeled 'scapegoats' too, tossed as we are into our own wilderness of Azazel. Yes? Never underestimate 'survivor guilt.' Yes? But of course, and happily, the courts went under, too, not only from the sheer weight of the litigants but, need I remind you, they're also under water now. So as to our being slapped with a subpoena, that seems unlikely today, scapegoats or not."

What am I doing with all this talk, talk, talk?

I used to be an artist. I was a painter. A surrealist. I had a modest following, collectors who would call me and come to visit my studio for a private view. Whatever it was in my imaginary painterly worlds that certain clients understood, I could depend upon those clients to purchase picture after picture.

No I was not made rich by the interest in my work. I was barely known. But I had my fans.

And with surrealism as my métier, it was no wonder it thrived in my small world; we lived in such surrealistic times. Anyone could recognize my metaphors. Water. Swimmers. Floating figures. Flying bird-women. Pregnant guardian angels.

Yet.

Yet when I produced a body of work that I called the 'goose-girl' series, I was puzzled at the vivid figures that grew on my canvases while under the influence of my inspiration. I was not sure where they had come from. Obviously, they were the products of my imagination, but in the sheer busy-ness of making the actual paintings — there were more than two dozen very large canvases, gallons of paint to mix, stretcher bars and yards of linen to be dealt with — I did not realize what the pictures were 'about.'

Now today I think I know.

And do I tell you? You, my imagined reader?

Use your imagination, dear reader. Think with yer butt, Flight Sergeant! And it will all be just tickety-boo.

In particular, I now see that the metaphors stand out clear and almost childlike in their directness, their simplicity. It's an interesting commentary on art and the world (if that's not too grand) that the metaphors are so obvious in the painting which forms the roof over the eastern deck of this treehouse. My pregnant, woman-goose-girl, pushing back at the very edges of her canvas world, powerful wings raised for flight.

"Oh Zelda, Mort. I am so, so tired."

I slumped over sideways and fell into agitated sleeping. I saw Wallace Barnaby, standing on my deck, on his hind legs, scanning the watery horizon. He was wearing those high-waisted, baggy and tapered Zoot Suit pants. Yellow gabardine. His front paws were tucked into his pants pockets, casual and confident and rakish, and on his head was set a diminutive red Pachuco Fedora, cocky, assertive.

—Elvis?—

I painted using a dry-brush technique. Fat bristled brushes dipped into pigment, punched almost dry on paper towels, then bounced onto my canvas. This technique created soft and cloudy color, transparent, and seeming to float. And if I bounced my dry brush one, two, three times, the color landed onto the fabric of the picture and, still transparent, floated, always revealing what was underneath the new color. Dry brush. And as the brush bounced upon the tightly-stretched canvas, it made a rhythmic thump, thump, thump. So lovely, the cadence to the addition of each layer of color.

But the subject matter?

A swimmer, diving backward, into, what? A wave? An ocean swimmer? A diver, immersed upside-down in deep clear water of translucent blue. A bird woman, wings spread in an enveloping atmosphere, flies. An argonaut in waters unfamiliar, with floating life-form companions.

Those were the things I might have wondered about.

But the bounce of my dry brush, thick stiff bristles, the thin spatters of color. Pounce. Pounce. Pounce. That was my work.

I was an artist, wordless.

Now?

Now I am what?

Survivor?

Householder?

Treehouse-holder?

Lone survivor? Well, maybe not now. There are others, I see.

I read. I clean my floor. I empty the outgoing. I get up. I see the sun. I mourn. I put raw fishes onto my tongue. I murder intruders. I survive.

If Sarah laughed, it was perhaps at the impossibility of giving birth at ninety.

If I laugh, it is at the impossibility of survival, at more than seventy-five years of age, in my treehouse.

It is simply unfathomable what has happened to our world, to me. Unfathomable. A fathom is six feet in water depth. And here I sit in my treehouse over how many fathoms I ask you? Not only is it incomprehensible, it is unfathomable, quite literally. Can't be measured. Can't be understood. Great watery pun. Perfection.

Sorry.

I am doing the best I can with my writing about events.

Really. I'm an artist after all.

Ah, well.

Back to the action!

I am typing now, recording the action as it today unfolds, in real time. My fingers tap the keyboard, pretty agile now after all the typing I have done so far from my treehouse. Tap, tap, tap, whomp, as I slug the carriage back, left to right, and tap, tap, tap, and whomp again.

Zelda and Mort have stuck with me throughout my detour with the scapegoats. They are stirring now. Shifting in their seats, legs numb perhaps, from sitting cross-legged on the deck throughout my sermon. Although I have noticed that Mort shifted a few times from padmasana to swasticasana to virasana.

Zelda starts on the response:

"You are wonderful, Sarah. Whether or not you are correct does not matter one bit. You make midrash seem like daily conversation. You make commentary on the thinking of the ancient rabbis. You tackle everything from ethics to justice. You give the heavens no quarter, nor any gods therein. Nor any wise men. You are a warrior. You are a bulldog. As Woody Allen once said, 'To the world I am an atheist. To God I am the loyal opposition.'"

Mort pipes up:

"Shall we recite another blessing ladies?"

Gently exasperated, Zelda replies:

"No, Mort. We shall not. Look at this girl. She's exhausted."

"It's true, Zelda. I am tapped out."

Ha! At least I've gotten past the water puns. Onward to typewriter puns!

I continue typing, bringing this to you, live, from high above the San Pablo Bay seasonal wetlands, this historic moment, the first observance of Rosh Hashanah from the treehouse of a lone survivor. Let's see what my guests, Rabbi Zelda Wurlitzer and Rabbi Mordachai Mendel are saying right now:

"Look Sarah. We need people like you. People who are not just surviving. But people alive enough to argue with God. To parse. To ask the difficult questions. To question every single previously accepted tennent of every single belief system. Even our own. Especially our own. Obviously, nothing works any more. And it's all been destroyed anyway. But has it really? You, Sarah Steinway, despite all your travails — maybe that's too grand — despite your circumstances, have stoked your anger and kept your curious mind active. Maybe that's how you have survived through all this shit. Can you recite the Kaddish Sarah?"

"Are you kidding, Zelda? What are you talking about?"

"Good. I thought so."

"Zelda! Are you crazy? Recite the ancient prayer over the dead? The dead we've had plenty. Not once have I said the Kaddish. You ask me, now, to pray?"

"Precisely, Sarah."

"Zelda, you are crazy. I have to clean the outgoing buckets. I have to catch Slow Fish. I need a nice hot bath. I am starving. I am hungry for brownies. Hell, I am hungry for a damned safety pin! And you want me to recite ancient useless words over dead bodies? Will God then give me a damn safety pin?"

"Sarah! Not because they are dead, the bodies that float past this treehouse. But because it's the right thing to do. And there's almost nobody left to do it. Kind of a rabbinic duty to serve, regardless of how futile the effort. It is not up to us to finish the task, but neither are we free to do nothing."

"Zelda, Zelda. I can't pray. It's all I can do to survive. I can't, I won't, I will not, I can NOT, pray."

At which point Mort jumps up, waving his arms and almost shouting:

"Zelda. Sarah. I must interrupt. Zelda, you are trying to get Sarah to take on the role of a post hoc rabbi. And Sarah, you fight this idea, the simple concept of prayer. Because you say you cannot pray. But you know what, Sarah? You know what, Zelda? This treehouse is your prayer Sarah. Fishing for Slow Fish is your prayer. Even cleaning the outgoing bucket is a form of prayer. Naming the Slow Fish is your prayer. Hacking the kudzu is your prayer. This work. Your work as a sole survivor, this work is the continuity practice of a very great yogi. Or of a very great mystical rabbi. You pray and you don't even know it. THIS…"

Mort flails his arms around in circles to include the room, the books, us.

"This is your prayer Sarah."

Hooboy.

I gotta stop typing.

Silence.

"Even typing is your prayer, Sarah. And your typewritten words are both midrash and commentary. Both. It's all prayer. So what's to harm with a little more prayer? Of saying simple syllables over the dead?"

"But there are not that many more dead at this point, Rabbi."

"All the more reason to say the Kaddish."

His reason did not sound reasonable to me.

There weren't any more reasons.

"You want I should serve my community in the role of a kind of eleventh hour rabbi. Not kosher, Rabbi, may I remind you. And community? What community?"

Zelda burst in:

"It's the right thing to do, Sarah."

"Sheesh, Zelda! Who's to care!?"

"We care. Mort and I."

"Great. All in favor? Done! Motion passed. This is ridiculous, rabbis."

We sit.

We had reached stasis. And now I could feel it shift. Entropy was setting in. The edifice of our mutual survival — this treehouse, my routines, my habits of survival — could not sustain the added weight of these other beings. Oh, not the weight of the additional bodies. God knows this treehouse was made to last, could bear any physical weight. But it, and I, could not bear the additional psychic weight. The close quarters alone would be enough to crush us all. There was only room for one of us here. For me. During these past few weeks, this treehouse had resisted our combined weights. The weight of forceful personalities. The weight of too many minds at work. The weight of terror and of work and of boredom. I, alone, in solitude — in my self-imposed solitary confinement — could bear those weights. And let me not forget, I could have avoided this entire set-up by having stayed uphill of The Emperor Tides when Epps and I drove some of my paintings to Placitas, New Mexico.

With Zelda and Mort, even with Wallace Barnaby and Laddy, we were like a family, infantilized by the propinquity of living together long after the kids were old enough to leave home. We would get mad or go mad. Whatever came next, we could not survive it if we tried to do so together.

"Listen, rabbis, Zelda, Mort, you, and Laddy, and Wallace Barnaby, you cannot stay here. It will be unbearable. We will all die trying to live together. You must leave for all of our sakes. You might just find high land and you can go about the business of argumentation with God with whomever washes up on that distant shore. But if you elect to stay here, it will sentence us all to, to, to. You see? I don't know."

So, they decided, that day, to go. And, once deciding, they left.

Rabbi Zelda Wurlitzer, Rabbi Mordachai Mendel, Wallace Barnaby, and Laddy Labradorian, swept down to the raft and quickly launched. Zelda employed the long pole to propel away from my tree. Rav Mort swept his blue-striped tallis around his body, picked up Wallace Barnaby, and tucked him inside its folds, close to his chest. Shipmates all of them. And they were gone.

Zelda was quick to obtain distance from the treehouse. Her outboard motor propelled the raft as she steered first east, then south, gathering momentum to find high ground. I watched them for a short while until they disappeared into a kind of mist, a regular San Francisco Bay fog.

But the hardest for me to watch leaving, was Rav Mort.

The last time I saw him, he had taken the most lovely revolved triangle pose on the deck of the raft. He, and Laddy, and Wallace Barnaby had struggled into Zelda's vessel with a bucket of Slow Fish, a plastic jug of water, and the pizza paddle, still too big and not big enough to make a good oar.

They could last a couple of days max, I figured, and only if they were not overwhelmed by waves from a new, and forceful, incoming tide.

Don't go, I thought. Don't. Yet I had launched them, as good as.

I was the one responsible for their leaving what little shelter I had provided for them. I watched the back of them. Rabbi Mort had brought his tallis over his own head and shoulders, and over Wallace Barnaby, and that was that. Whatever protection the sanctified fringed scarf offered them was purely irrational, purely to do with God and Mort. And that kind of protection did not figure for much in this particular dire strait. I had seen the flood take the righteous and the opposite sort. We were all damned. And doomed.

Two days after they had struck off, I scuffed out onto the deck, stood there holding onto the handrail facing east looking across what was 'water, water everywhere' just to see what I could see. I was numb. Indifferent. Who cares what I can see? Not even I care. But it was something to do.

But there was something. What was it? I raised my binoculars.

There was a blue and white bundle wrapped around a body and long floating fringes waving in the placid outgoing tide. I jumped, almost dropped the binoculars and they thumped, anticlimactic and disastrous, against the railing. I heard glass break. Looking through them again, I saw that one lens was cracked. Little bits of glass tinkled onto the platform at my feet. But the other lens was okay, just. The blue and white bundle, wrapped in Rabbi Mort's tallis, was making an arc in the tidal waters, slowly forming what I saw was to be a gigantic, swirling 'C' that would end at or near my treehouse. The fringes dragged along behind and formed curls and loops on the surface of the moving water.

God, oh God. I would need to say the Kaddish. Just speak the words. Do it. It is the right thing to do.

I started to say the words. Only I was so nervous and confused, and my mind was crazy with too much, just too much, death, drowning, water, Slow Fish, solitude. If I had gone quite mad, who was there to care or criticize or, for that matter, who would there be to say Kaddish over my dead self? And so I began:

Yitgadal v'yitkadash sh'mei raba.

B'alma di v'ra chirutei,

v'yamlich malchutei,

b'chayeichon uv'yomeichon

uv'chayei d'chol beit Yisrael,

baagala uviz'man kariv. V'im'ru: Amen.

Y'hei sh'mei raba m'varach

l'alam ul'almei almaya.

Yitbarach v'yishtabach v'yitpaar

v'yitromam v'yitnasei,

v'yit'hadar v'yitaleh v'yit'halal

sh'mei d'kud'sha b'rich hu,
l'eila min kol birchata v'shirata,
tushb'chata v'nechemata,
daamiran b'alma. V'imru: Amen.

Y'hei sh'lama raba min sh'maya,
v'chayim aleinu v'al kol Yisrael.
V'imru: Amen.

Oseh shalom bimromav,
Hu yaaseh shalom aleinu,
v'al kol Yisrael. V'imru: Amen.

Exalted and hallowed be God's great name
in the world which God created, according to plan.
May God's majesty be revealed in the days of our lifetime
and the life of all Israel — speedily, imminently, to which we
say Amen.

Blessed be God's great name to all eternity.
Blessed, praised, honored, exalted, extolled, glorified, adored,
and lauded be the name of the Holy Blessed One, beyond all
earthly words and songs of blessing, praise, and comfort. To
which we say Amen.

May there be abundant peace from heaven, and life, for us
and all Israel, to which we say Amen.

May the One who creates harmony on high, bring peace to

us and to all Israel. To which we say Amen.

And the bundle, bundled in its tallis, floated just near enough for me to reach forward and grab a fistful of the fringe and pull it so that it floated to rest, at last, against the trunk of my tree. I carefully pulled the edges back from the head, first this side, then that side, waterlogged, muddy, the blue stripes indecipherable from the mud and algae and water.

It was Wallace. Wally Walleye. Wallace Barnaby.

I am furious. I shout to the unseen presence:

"See what happens when you make a rabbi out of a sow's ear. Mistakes are made. And now a cat, Wallace Barnaby, is assured comfort in the world to come. And Rabbi Mort, the bodhisattva of rabbis, is still out there floating through the cosmos, victim number one gazillion, of The Emperor Floods and without a word of comfort he heard. I am a failure as a rabbi. That's what you get Zelda Wurlitzer!"

```
                     -VIII-
        Watch out for the government . . .
              they do not stand by
           a person who is in distress.


                  Pirke Avot 2:3
```

IT WAS A DRONE.

I could see that with my binoculars. Its distinctive dull smooth profile. Black underbelly, sky blue upper fuselage, wings bent into a downward facing V. Black bird. 'Black bird singing at the break of day. Take these broken wings and learn to fly.'

It hovered here and there, aiming a long cylindrical object in the direction of various outcroppings of mud and plastic sky-scrapers. Moving slowly, it headed toward the kudzu island about a mile away. The tendrils of the plant snapped — hungry, vora-cious, attracted to the body heat of the aircraft, I suppose. The drone drew back, graceful, seemingly effortlessly and continued, lazily, on its mission, whatever that would turn out to be.

I kept watching from my deck.

Then it maneuvered leisurely — silent and weird — bobbing

this way and that way as if distracted by various outcroppings and objects that it passed, but it moved steadily, if slowly, heading in my direction, heading for my treehouse.

I ducked down, uselessly. What was the point really?

It was easy to watch it with my daytime binoculars. Broken as they were, I could still make out features and details on the drone fuselage. A flag? Was that the flag of a country? Numbers? But not numbers I recognized. Maybe Greek alphabet letters? As it droned closer, I put the binoculars down and just watched it — it hypnotized me — so out of context over these dark waters; sleek, and man made, and sinister.

Now, it was close enough to my treehouse, to my body, to unnerve me. I patted my hair into place, reflexively, as if I were in front of a hallway mirror, getting ready to receive guests. This militaristic, surrealistic aircraft was about to perform an intervention into my private, mad, suffering, and beloved world, into the world of my treehouse.

Gracefully, it maneuvered with a little hovering bounce, coming to a halt sideways in front of me, in full profile. Now I could read the words on the side.

ARCH-A-PELA-GO! AIR AND WATER TAXI SERVICE.

And then, the logo, elaborate script with backwards and forwards facing 'Es.'

Men and their machines. God love 'em!

"Epps? Is that you?"

A mechanical voice responded:

"Insert identifying paperwork in front of view finder."

"What? What are you talking? Epps?"

"Place identifying paperwork into view finder in front of

exterior camera."

"Are you kidding?"

I raced back inside and flung open my waterproof safe, digging deep into its scattered and torn reminiscences: old photos, a baby shoe, my birth certificate, a ring and, there! The Emanuel Epps LLP letterhead entitled Steinway Treehouse: Expenses. Torn, moldy, bug eaten, barely readable, there it was in a little plastic sleeve I had put it in all those years ago. I stumbled back onto my deck, waving it, waving it somewhere near what I took to be the viewpoint of a camera, that long cylindrical object I had observed as the drone had flown closer.

Activated, the camera dived toward my paperwork, swiveled to change lenses, drew forward again until it was almost touching the letterhead. It scanned, swiftly, left to right, side to side, as if it were reading. And then I heard:

"Sarah?"

And again:

"Sarah Steinway? As in piano?"

And then:

"Is that you Sarah?"

"No you idiot. It's Marilyn Monroe! Who-the-fuck do you think it is? You, you, you overweening, pompous, smug, vain, vainglorious, foolish, foolish man. Epps! Is that YOU?"

A longish silence. Then I heard:

"Handrails. No finials!"

"Right! That's right, Epps. And look at me now. Alive to tell it. Alive to tell it. No finials."

"Sarah! You are alive. You look terrible!"

"Thank you, Epps. Always with the flattery."

After all I have endured? And he comments on my appearance, my looks?

It all boils down to how I look?

I, reflexively, touch my neck.

How did I look after all this time living above these waters? He was utterly adorable, but, 'Oink' however, on this topic! I fired off:

"Well, how the hell do you think I look, Epps? How do you think I look? How do I look after digesting the filthy, inedible leavings of a drowned world? How do I look after sickness, blindness, cold bitterness? How do I look after suffering bleak lonesome endless dead silence, after raving inside my own crazy brain, after insanity, after murder, after floundering then failing to even be able to recite the words of comfort for the dead, therefore abrogating my meagre faux-rabbinic responsibilities? I have failed everything, everything: health, honor, bravery. The only success I have endured is my own longevity. How do I look? Look at me. THIS is how I look."

"It's been years, Sarah."

"So?"

"Sarah. We, we could have been, Sarah Steinway. We could have been."

"Well, if you expect me to respond to this chick lit ending you are sadly wrong, my errant friend. Finials or no finials. I am not leaving this treehouse."

"Sarah! Are you crazy? Are you nuts? Do you have any idea what's been happening?"

"I don't know and I don't care. I am not leaving this treehouse."

"Don't be a fool, Sarah. The only thing remaining in former

sea level lands is a scattered archipelago of higher-altitude islands. And I, you will be thrilled to note, run and operate a very lucrative water and air taxi service between these water-logged formations. You could not ask for a better helpmeet than me, Emanuel Epps. We could make a life, Sarah. We could have our old life back."

"What life, Epps? This. This is my life. I made this life, and I'm sticking to it."

"You, Sarah Steinway, are an impossible woman."

"Not to change the subject, Epps, but what became of Hampton, Ruggles and Sterns?"

I hear him sigh.

"Impossible woman! Eugene Hampton found a circuitous route uphill and got his Ph.D. New thesis: Poetry of The Emperor Tides. Huge hit. Cum Laude, and all that. Ruggles is the Republican Representative of the new U.S. Southern Rebs Archipelago. Same damn agenda, Sarah. Drives me nuts. And Jerry Sterns…"

Epps pauses. I hear him take a breath and blow it out. Cigarette? Dope?

"Jerry Sterns was one of the first casualties. Tore off going east. That bigfoot truck of his got swamped by one of those first really fierce incoming tides and, glug, glug, he's a goner."

"I am sorry to hear that, Epps. He saved my life, you know. With all that survival stuff. A lot of foresight in all that. And it worked. Works, I should say. Even those freakish Hunter's Friend Oak Tree costumes turned out to provide warmth in the cold of the fog."

We were silent for a moment. Me standing on my deck, and

Epps encased somewhere, probably at quite a distance, maneuvering his drone. I heard Sterns in my mind:

"I will NOT be up shit creek without the proverbial. Mark my words Sarah."

And I had.

"So, you want to make a new life, Sarah?"

"You mean your standard chick lit ending?"

"Sarah, Sarah! You are an impossible woman."

I pulled rank:

"Rabbi, to you, Epps."

"I know."

"What, you know?"

"A raft washed up on one of the outliers. A woman and a man — couple of rabbis they told me. Rabbi Zelda Wurlitzer, I think, and Rav Mort Mendel. She told me all about it. And about you. How do you think I got the notion to come out here in the first place? And it is NOT a chick lit ending. It's just me. Epps. Wouldn't you rather live life annoying the hell out of each other — together — than annoying each other apart? And, besides. The whole world's gone to hell in a handbasket. If you were a skeptical, glass-half-empty-type person, you might just say it's a living hell out here. Some chick lit ending that would be, Sarah."

"Always the charmer. You talk a good line. No dice. You see, Epps, I am just fine living apart from you. I am happy, even."

Silence. The drone shifted sideways then faced me frontwise. And I saw that there was a smiley face painted on its nosecone.

"Oh for heaven's sakes! Epps, you are crazy."

"You'll be okay then, Sarah?"

"Okay. Yes. I will be very okay. I am very okay."

Then the drone pulled up closer for a second, and a bay door opened, and from that a disembodied mechanical hand, holding a raggedy burlap bag, reached outside and dropped the bag, point blank, onto my deck.

It landed with a rattling thump.

Then the craft veered off suddenly, flying fast and south.

I went over to the parcel. It was fastened with twine and attached to the twine was a piece of cardboard with hand-lettered words:

Air Epps.

Your supplies delivered to you direct.

No island too small or too distant.

Just remember Archa-pela-Go!

And the logo: backwards and forwards facing Es.

I pulled off the twine, coiling it into a tidy circle around my fingertips. It could be useful for later. And I peered down into the sack.

Finials. It was a bag of finials.

I dumped them out onto the deck. Out flopped a packet of grubby, folded papers. I grabbed them just as a gust of wind was about to grab them from me.

There were six or seven sheets of dirty bond paper, creased so thoroughly that the folds were starting to rub thin. The letter was written in blunt pencil on the backs of old Emanuel Epps

LLC letterheads entitled: Additional Expenses Steinway Tree-house. And here is what it read:

Dear Sarah Dear,

You would not believe what has been going on out here.

After leaving you in your lair, is that too fancy? How 'bout, in your nest, maybe better. After leaving you that evening, off into the sunset went I. Nice touch, eh? I motored north then inland and uphill, ending in Montana, and not before a stint in the Rockies, big mistake, remember the Donner Party? Well, I made it, and limped along south again, a spoonful of petrol here, a spoonful there, ending at my summer home, remember the book jackets with: He divides his time between San Francisco and Santa Fe — as if — and finally, I had to walk the bike up the hill to the little house, faux adobe, sitting facing west here in Placitas New Mexico. Remember that trip you and I made to deposit your life work in my garage? Well, the house is still here. And your paintings are still here. Dusty, but okay. Your paintings are destined for art history. You glad?

It is perhaps no great surprise that, with the migration of thousands of people fleeing the lowlands and the threatening Emperor Tides, that, soon, civil disarray set in throughout New Mexico. It happened at first slowly and without much notice because there were so many catastrophes, small and large, that occurred every day. Power outages. Burning automobiles. Lost pets. Fistfights. Hey, babies were even born! But at last you had to realize, if you were not a complete idiot, that the situation was very bad.

Sarah are you listening? Well, get this.

You know, before the flood, Placitas, New Mexico had been a retirement destination for many army and air force and navy officers and their wives. New Mexico was, for the retired military families, an attractive respite after serving their country in many faraway lands. These men had organizational skills and strategic and analytic training. So they gathered together after the various catastrophes and the flood and all, to cobble a civilian guardian force as the threats and dangers of The Emperor Tides increased and as the local population swelled with lowlands people fleeing for their lives uphill, to New Mexico, elevation 5,200 feet.

The retired military commanders conducted meetings with each neighborhood group, assembling as many people as possible and organizing them into subgroups. It could not have been easy because most of us had not had military careers. We were an odd assortment of aging retirees from Chicago, Los Angeles, San Francisco, Minneapolis, from all over the place. You had, in our numbers, more than the usual physical limitations as the median age was around 73. There was an abundance of the technologies of old age; dozens of titanium knees and hips, scores of heart stents and hearing aids. And, there were all of the usual nascent diseases of our lot. Hiding in the interstices of these old bodies were the usual plagues of old age: cancers, fibrillations, anoxia, kidney failure, brain aneurisms, and senile dementias of every variety, sleeplessness, anxiety, and rampant crankiness. A mighty band of soldiers we were not. It must have been hard on the generals when they stepped up to help these little communities, to organize them and to train them in the rudiments of self-protection. A hopeless task, you know, Sarah. And so there was formed a kind of mock-military made up of the halt and the lame and every few days one of us would die of something or other. There were only two retired doctors in the whole of Placitas. It was all you could do to keep up with the burials. But we did. You dug holes in the rocky soil. You sniffled by the graveside. You honored the fallen. It was the right thing to do, I guess.

The rest of the world was gone. Berserk!

Civilization died with the influx from sea level of people fleeing in panic and hunger and frustration and fear. This led to chaos. For example: Every edible morsel contained the latency of murder. People killed one another, men and women, old and young, and teenagers and even small children, they, all of them, would fight, ungainly and ugly, scratching, kicking, screaming, they would wrestle, clumsy and inept; they would fight, to the death for a rotting apricot.

Hunger also drove people to shoot New Mexico coyotes and bobcats. Guns, they had plenty. God bless the second amendment! Then, after several months of that kind of killing, the hunters discovered the empty animal dens that were scattered along the arroyos. You saw human beings, dirty and bloody, curled around their weapons, nestled inside those stony caves. Feral and sated, squatters now, these hunters were living in the very homes of the animals they had murdered to eat. Not pretty, Sarah.

There were also weird outside forces. Over our heads flew drones, all kinds of drones and almost every day and sometimes even after dark. These craft included some that appeared to be home-made and some that projected the sleek lineage of ex-military weapons. Some strafed or bombed the foothills and arroyos.

They killed or maimed men. Used as target practice domestic animals, cats and dogs. There were no identifying graphics on the most sophisticated of the drones. God knows what country or entity or corporation they represented. But the deal was, drones most often killed anyone in their jutting pathways. Soon enough, you get inured to their dangers. You just continue about your business, the business of not dying, of not being killed, of eating something, of being sick in the roadway, and the irony of striving not to die was that the drones represented almost certain death and you simply ignored them.

One set of drones even provided a modicum of entertainment for us. The Gnome Drones. Some techie wag had made flying vehicles out of garden gnomes. They bobbled and dipped haphazardly, not being very aerodynamic. So you'd look at an approaching flying object and soon realize, it's a gnome! And here it comes! And seeing it, you'd laugh; how could you not? And then, the gnome's beady eyes right in front of your face, a tiny deadly weapon would telescope out from the gnome's little green jacket and, well, blam, you're dead. But not before you'd had your last laugh.

Many of us realized that, as single and aged people, you would not last long out here without help. I had a couple of buddies, Vietnam vets, both well over seventy years and I invited them to help me survive in exchange for food from my hidden stash. You know: the stuff in my studio sub-basement.

There was something military in the air and it caught on in the formation of many small bands of people. Rebels? Insurgents? Revolutionaries? Nothing of the sort. There were no doctrines, no ideals, no political content to the need for these lit-

tle aging gangs. You didn't rationally consider anything in those days. There was not time. Nor energy. Everything was ad hoc. Regular ad-hocksters, us. You just did what had to be done to survive. And so you gathered a sort of Praetorian Guard into your household: old vets, homeless widows, the lonely, the bewildered and you continued to live life as best as you could. After a couple of years, you had gathered quite a bedraggled, yet oddly bonded, little family.

Our Placitas population diminished over the years of the civil disarray. Yet, several hundred out of the original several thousands, had made it through those five years. And even among the very aged, there were survivors who seemed to have been fortified, actually, by their trials.

Well, Sarah, that's about it. I got work to do. Gotta keep the enterprises going. As you see I nabbed one of those drones and its work, work, work for me. You need anything, send up a flair. Better yet, I will check in every once in a while.

And so it is just this: We are grateful to see this day. If I told you what is really going on, you, and I, would go mad. I mean; it's worse, much worse.

So, instead, I tell you I love you Sarah. But not like that.
All best, Epps

Vain. Vainglorious, little man.
Vain!
Glorious!

-IX-

Against your will were you born.

Against your will,

you live.

Against your will,

you will die.

Pirke Avot 4:22

I am much like my famous Torah namesake, Sarah. The first Sarah. She bore a child in her nineties, a very old woman. And that child was to give life to a nation. I built a treehouse as a very old woman. And it was to give life to me. I gave life to it and it provided life for me. *Quid pro quo. La dor v'dor.*

So let's hear it for the Sarahs! Old women, both.

But.

There is always a 'but'. Here's my 'but'. It's a beef. And it goes like this:

After surviving various catastrophes — things like cancer or car wrecks, or earthquakes — let's say the drug performed a miracle; the passengers climbed out of the wreckage without a scratch; the beam fell just two inches away from your head — after surviving these kinds of things, sometimes, people say that they 'found God' as a result.

Not so here. In my case.

I had hoped, vain hope, crazy talk, that God, He, She or It, would have — for God's sake! — would have found ME!

But no.

Did you know that our scriptures do not include a single word from the mouth of our original Sarah? Were her words and thoughts merely edited out of the plot? Were her words and thoughts not considered to be valuable when the councils of men assembled to edit the cherished books? Why was she left out?

Well, unlike my namesake Sarah, I will not be left out of my own story.

I am not that Sarah.

I, Sarah Steinway, will not be edited out, if that, indeed, is what happened to my namesake. If you want to know what this Sarah thought, what I thought and felt, and what labor I bore during this birthing of my tree home, and of my 'survivor-self,' then you can read all about it, here, in these pages.

And so my life alone ends.

Did I actually think I could survive this thing forever?

To tell the truth, I did not think one thing or another. Except to finish my treehouse. That, I had wanted to do. So that I could have a place where I could think, alone. Without interruptions. With no Internet. No barking dogs. No doorbells. But so very much thinking? And so very much of being alone?

This would be my last night sleeping here, alone, at home in my treehouse.

Now I lay me down to sleep.

The treehouse is tight. On this last night as lone survivor, I appreciate its steadfastness.

The tree groans with the hydraulic force of the lapping tide. I hear loud snaps of wood under pressure and softer squeaks like old wood floorboards under foot. The massive upper limbs of my tree play a wooden tune against the wind, and the cabling harps a sonorous song in a minor key. Fog rolls in around the leaves, and I hear them drip. The tree embraces me.

Lying on my futon, I put my ear against the floorboards and listen. My ear, like a stethoscope, picks up the beating heart of my little house. Home. I hear little pops of wood in expansion and contraction. Life, alone, for me, sole, began with dreaming.

Am I dreaming now?

One strange thing I am grateful for is that a mirror Epps and I had struggled to install during a moment of low tides, fell to the ground and smashed. I was left with a single viciously pointed triangular shard, large enough for my face to fit onto, with my cheekbones tangent on two of the three jagged edges of the mirror. But this mirror was not so large that I could ever get far enough away to see my whole body. So mornings I would look into my shard, which stood against a group of books on the shelf, the works of Colette I believe and, yes, I was still there. As I write — type rather — at this moment, several seasons have passed and now I am as wrinkled as a dried fig, dark, sere, and wary. My eyes are feral and red-rimmed above the press of my own sharpened cheekbones. Who is fairest of them all?

Who am I?

Who have I been?

You know, you can only know anything about yourself by looking back, not by looking into a mirror, no, but only by looking backwards through your life can you know who you have been and, extrapolating, who you are.

Not in the moments that things, and events, and people, and love, and parents, and pets — not in the moments when all of those converge, haphazard and too fast — can you know what it all means. The themes. The reasons why. The thrilling conclusion. The denouement. None of those are evident except when looking backwards.

You?

You see what I mean.

I still talk to an omnipresent other, to a 'you'.

Is that 'you' God?

Silence.

Surely not.

You let me go through all of this and not a peep?

See what I mean?

I may have tried, but other than the prayer of my survival, the ordinary acts — clean the buckets, scoop the fishes — the rabbis got that right. My survival, then, has been my prayer.

So, here's a last tidbit: As an artist, I was used to long hours alone, painting. Was never lonesome when alone. So now I see how being a painter prepared me for hours alone being a sole-survivor. I was in training, back then, alone, with my canvas, my brushes, my pots of paint. And now I see, looking backwards, how my painting was my prayer. Score another one for the rabbis.

There was nothing else to do but to survive.

I mean: end of the world and all.

Then this: ever so slightly embarrassed, I turned to Torah. Feeling a bit sheepish, I turned to Torah for comfort. I felt certain

I would die, so I turned to scripture.

Except for this: Me being secular and all, I made commentary — or midrash — on the stories, filling them in when I felt that something was missing. And that probably kept my brain cells functioning.

I mean, looking back now, I see how I have been just an ordinary woman, with ordinary middlebrow expectations of life. To love. To accept love. To do a pretty okay job with my life. Not to seek fame. Not to flee it either. Just ordinary hopes. And then: I was called upon to survive. No. That's too grand. I just did it. I survived.

I did it in this strange land of no-land, of only water. A stranger in this strange diaspora. I survived as did my ancestors, I guess. I, Sarah Steinway. Somehow, I got tapped — or thumped? — by God, by He, She or It, to carry out the historic survival of my people. Is that too grand?

I am sitting here on the floor of my deck and the sun appears to rise above the horizon of water. The sun's brightness scatters over fresh water today, and the new water flows and sloshes, benign, beneath the floor of my treehouse. This is a gentle tide of clear, transparent, turquoise water. It is clear, and turquoise, and flows, languid, liquid, and I can see into the deep water for yards around the base of my treehouse. And beneath about fifteen feet of this clear blue water I see the topmost angle of my Taliesin house roofline, a right angle set at an angle. And along the edges of that roofline, I see here and there, clinging to the fascia boards, branches of red coral. And around the coral branches swim orange and yellow angelic fishes with trailing scarves of red chiffon. And I see ruffled, blue-finned fishes waving capes, and their tiny sequined vests glimmer in the shafts of sunlight that penetrate the bright blue waters. I creep along my deck on my butt to get a closer look, and I see beneath the clear-flowing tide that the entire roofline and, God knows, the whole house probably, is draped in a vivid undulating green algae bloom, vivid chartreuse angel hair, like springtime grasses, several feet in length and clinging to every surface of my house. And around this waving algae swim Slow Fish in their thousands, golden finned today and bright eyed. Submerged beneath the tranquil turquoise water, the roofline, the parapets, the shingles, the stucco of my Taliesin house, are all draped with a growth of algae, and it flows and undulates in lazy strokes, this way and that way, moving with the incoming tide, and the water is clear, and transparent, and gentle. And there is a world of living activity down there where my house now resides under water. There are sea creatures of all kinds. Purple, spiny puffer fish jut between lavender sea anemones, and a lazy flat fish blinks at me with long cerulean eyelashes and there is a dappled octopus flashing first purple, then orange, then magenta. Its limbs animate into pinto patterns as it feels its way among the flowing algae grasses. And under the bloom of grassy threadlike algae and the activity of all those convivial creatures of the deep, lies my Taliesin house. My home.

How to fathom this?

I do not know.

You are reading this because you found a five-gallon plastic water bottle floating atop endless black waters in the ocean.

Or.

You are reading this because you found a five-gallon plastic water bottle wedged into a dry bank of an ancient mudflat in a desert mesa that used to be an ocean.

I place these pages into a five-gallon water container and set them into this rising tide to live a life of their own. I will never know if they survive.

But I did.

I survived.

Now it's sink or swim. I place these pages into a vessel and set them free. Sink or swim little words I pray. Off you go.

I am so

Note to readers: Sarah's typing breaks off here.

Annex to Sarah's Treehouse

I met Sarah Steinway fifty years ago in college. She usually sat in the back row of the art history lectures. I don't remember her saying a single word in class back then. But she could talk, alright, lecture even, sometimes madly hectoring. Looking back on those times, I see now that Sarah was self-confident without being very self-aware. I did not know her, really. We were not friends back then.

Years passed.

Then suddenly she came back into my life.

It was as if Sarah had appeared out of nowhere. One minute she was not. The next minute she was here: mouthy, reticent yet edgy, a skeptic, always with the argument, railing to God, passionately not believing one minute, then, as urgently, passionate in prayer.

At that point, she and I could have been friends.

She and my neighbor, Emanuel Epps, had come out to Placitas to stash some of her paintings in his garage. Sea levels along the California coast were rising and Sarah was afraid her paintings would be drowned. Instead of staying here, they turned around, and drove back to the San Pablo Bay seasonal wetlands.

Again, years passed.

After The Emperor Floods, I met Sarah's friends, the rabbis Zelda Wurlitzer and Mordechai Mendel. They simply trudged uphill and knocked on my door. And that is how I came to possess a five-gallon water bottle, crammed with Sarah's narration of survival in her treehouse.

The water bottle had floated up to the rabbis' raft. They recognized the bottle from their stay in Sarah's treehouse. Zelda hooked it with her long pole and they kept it on board. Later their barge crashed onto the western border of New Mexico, the new seashore after sea levels had risen. The two rabbis and their stash of Sarah's words survived the crash.

Sarah grew out of memories.

Someone waved his arms and said: "This, this, is your prayer."

And someone said: "You have your whole life ahead of you."

And someone said: "We opened the cockpit doors."

And someone said: "Do it because it is the right thing to do."

And someone said: "Who shall live and who shall die?"

And Sarah said: "My name is Sarah Steinway. As in piano."

Along with these typewritten pages, there are a few incidental pieces: poems, snippets, unfinished sentences, little sketches. The typed pages, Sarah's story, were stained and dirty, some showing signs of having been immersed in muddy waters. I had them typeset at a little print shop located in a garage in what remains of Placitas, New Mexico. The enterprise, run by Emanuel Epps, operates beneath a hand-painted sign that reads:

EMANUEL EPPS - JUST YOUR TYPE

Epps and I sorted and edited Sarah's typewritten pages as best we could, then bound them into the book you have here in your hands. It's not perfect, but it's okay for now.

As I read her typewritten pages, it is as if she were poking at my sternum with two unbent fingers saying: Are you listening? Do you hear me?

Not only did she live, but she insisted upon it.

Good-bye, Sarah Steinway. As in piano.

—End—

Acknowledgements

Grateful thank you for your patience and insights, my first readers: Norma Libman, Nancie Gilbert, Elizabeth DuFrane, Julie Denison, Sharon Baker, Rabbi Deborah J. Brin and Rabbi Jack Shlachter.

For mechanical information about the effects of wind and weather on Cessna aircraft fuselages and wings, and upon their pilots, thank you Doug Morris. For technical information about firearms, thank you Floyd Cotton.

Faber Academy's Full Manuscript Evaluations were excellent and helped me enormously. Thank you to the staff and to the reader who encouraged me in shaping this work.

To my editor, Allison Smith, thank you; the book would not have happened without your enthusiasm.

And grateful thanks and love to Gary W. Priester, husband and best friend ever, for more than forty years.

This book is my love letter to my Taliesin-inspired home, designed and built by architect Thomas Bingham, who studied architecture at Taliesin West with Frank Lloyd Wright. That house, our home for sixteen years, was located overlooking the San Pablo Bay seasonal wetlands.

Mary E. Carter
2018
Placitas, New Mexico, USA

Mary E. Carter was born in the San Fernando Valley of orange groves and dirt roads. Most of her life she lived and worked in California and had a long career as an advertising copywriter and graphic designer. She now lives in New Mexico where she paints and writes. Her memoir, *A Non-Swimmer Considers Her Mikvah*, was a 2016 WINNER in the New Mexico-Arizona Book Awards. Her first book, *Electronic Highway Robbery* was published by Peachpit Press in 1996. *I, Sarah Steinway* is her first novel.

This book is my love letter to my Taliesin-inspired home, designed and built by architect Thomas Bingham, who studied architecture at Taliesin West with Frank Lloyd Wright.

OCT 13 2020